DARK ORCHIDS

by

Zana Etter

ISBN-13 978-0692274293

ISBN-10 0692274294

Acknowledgments

The author wishes to thank the Blue Moon Writers Group for insightful, perceptive comments and support many years ago when this story first took shape.

Special thanks to my editor, Nikki Busch, for constructive, tactful help in perfecting details, and adhering to accepted practice and publishing formats.

Thanks also to Robert Helmbrecht, Librarian at the Hillsborough, New Jersey Public Library, for invaluable assistance in formatting the work in preparation for submission to be published.

I dedicate this book to my mother who was my first "reader" and who provided me with suggestions, and to my father, whose writing ability I think I inherited, making this work possible.

Thanks to all my friends who encouraged me, my husband who supported my efforts, and my son. I hope he will someday see his mother's name on many book titles in a rack at an airport shop, when he is on his way to a gate to check in as a pilot.

March 1990

DARK ORCHIDS

PROLOGUE

Roberto Santiago slammed his foot down on the brake and parked the Lada in front of the bar. He jumped out and pushed open the frosted glass doors and walked through the smoky, noisy crowd. Finding the counter at the back of the room, he quickly sat down and ordered a beer. As soon as it came, he began to gulp the cool liquid. Suddenly he felt a hand slap his back. He turned around and glared at his brother-in-law.

"Why did you follow me here, Carlos? I told you I am not interested in working for you."

"You dare to turn me down after all I did for your sister?"

"I told you I will never dirty my hands working for you. I don't believe in what you are doing. My father isn't strong enough to fight you, but I am!"

"Fight *me*? You will never win. I don't like to be told no, and I get even with those who oppose me."

"Is that a threat? My sister was a fool to marry you! You have made her life miserable and ruined my father's." Roberto glared at Carlos and swung a punch, knocking him to the floor. Kicking him once, he pulled him to his feet.

"Leave me alone for the last time, Carlos. Get out of here!"

Carlos shot him an angry look and turned to go.

"This will be the last time you see me, Roberto." He walked slowly away and out the door.

Roberto ordered another beer and then another. At 4 a.m. he staggered out to his car and closed the door, remembering to lock it. He pushed the key in and turned it. The sudden blast broke the frosted glass bar doors and sprayed metal and blood and arms into the air—they landed on the deserted street and sidewalk.

May 1990

CHAPTER 1

Paul Brennan squinted into the bright sunlight, as he looked out over the ocean from his hotel balcony and reached for his sunglasses. Taking the coffee cup from the breakfast tray, he moved to the ledge and looked down toward the harbor. Ferries plied their way back and forth, making the small sailboats and fishing rigs tilt and bob in their wake. An incoming seaplane glided to a stop while a ship's horn announced the approach of a white, multi-tiered goddess, spewing grey smoke through her black stacks, sliding through the mountain pass on her way to St. Thomas's bustling dock.

Swallowing the sweet hot latte to help him stay alert, the journalist gazed upward at the lush, green-covered mountain peaks surrounding the island. In the hazy distance to the left, he could just discern the flat, brown island with the tiny peak called a French cap. The warm breeze blew his light brown hair back off his forehead, and birdcalls, foghorns, and plane engines melted into an island song trying to lull him back to sleep. He began to think of his last assignment and of the colleague he'd left in Kashmir.

A sharp knock at the door abruptly broke his reverie. He left the balcony and walked to the hotel room door. Reaching for the latch, he heard the melodic, high-pitched voice of the maid on his floor.

"Monsieur Brennan, it is Clotilde. I have a..." She abruptly stopped talking when he opened the door. In a lower voice she almost whispered, "A gentleman in the coffee bar downstairs told me to give this to you. I come back soon to clean your room." Handing him a note, she quickly turned and went down the hall. Paul closed the door and opened the folded paper.

"Meet me at twelve o'clock on French cap. Come alone. Get boat off pier at Calalou Street."

No signature. He went out into the hall to look for the maid, but she was gone. She had left her cart at the other end of the corridor. Searching for her, he peered into every open door on the floor, but she had disappeared. He wanted to get a description of the person who had given her the note. Reluctantly he returned to his room, showered, dressed, and headed downtown.

Leaving the hotel, he found himself in the dusty narrow streets, passing the women going home from working the night shift, their colorful, plaid bandanas pressed to sweaty foreheads, hiding hair that needed to be shampooed. They chattered happily in time to the flop and click of their wooden sandals against the dry, hardened skin of their tired, blistered feet. They disappeared around a corner, probably to a crowded house where they had children waiting to be fed and a husband eager to leave for work or perhaps the local bar.

Once he crossed the wide boulevard, the trash-littered streets became filled with tourists from the cruise ships, their white shopping bags bulging ahead of them. Walking across the cobblestoned path, which bordered the edge of the pier, he scanned the docks hoping to spot a local fisherman or boat captain. Most of the boats were still out gathering the morning catch or had been chartered by private groups for snorkeling runs.

Pacing back and forth, he pulled out the note and reread the words, trying to imagine the mystery writer. He tucked it back into his shirt pocket, and suddenly felt a presence behind him, as if someone was trying to peer over his shoulder. Smelling the distinct odor of rum mingled with sweat, and feeling hot breath near his ear, he spun around to see a thin, wiry islander, his tanned and weather-worn face telling him at once he had found his fisherman. The man's twinkling blue eyes kept darting up and down and then away toward the docks.

"Need a boat?" he asked rapidly in perfect English.

8

"Well, I'd like to see French cap if that's possible. I have some free time."

"There isn't much to see over there. Just tall grass and wild goats.

"How long would it take to get there?"

"Not long…thirty minutes…for a price," he announced in a lower voice, his bright eyes gleaming.

Paul pulled out two crisp twenty dollar bills and waved them in front of his tanned, little nose, but the fisherman pushed the hand away.

"Okay…clip too!"

The journalist removed the gold-filled money clip he used to keep his American currency separate from the local bills. He pushed the clip and money into the man's brown, wrinkled hand and the fisherman sprang ahead, almost running toward the docks. Paul followed him about a quarter of a mile until the shore curved and became an inlet. All the while the fisherman smoked furiously and muttered strange words. Not wanting to distract him and glad to have found someone to take him across the bay, Paul asked no questions as he tried to keep up with him.

Finally they came upon a small boat tied to a post. The fisherman quickly untied the vessel and pulled the cord to start the motor. He jumped in and Paul stepped in carefully. Suddenly they sped off. As Paul looked back at the shore, the dock grew smaller and the water became choppy, making the salt water fly up to sting his face. The wind, which was soft and gentle onshore, became untamed and forceful, and he pulled his cap down lower over his forehead. The sun was almost overhead now, knifing its hot rays into the top of his skull. As the navigator deftly maneuvered his craft in the island's direction, Paul wondered if he would require more payment for the return trip. All he had of value was his watch and a silver belt buckle, unless the fisherman fancied famous-label polo shirts!

Suddenly the fisherman cut the motor, and they drifted along slowly, almost silently. The fisherman appeared apprehensive as he turned his head back and forth for a while, listening intently to the sounds of the sea. Gulls flew over their heads and a buoy bobbed and clanged. Then Paul saw French cap loom into view off the port side and the fisherman turned the boat toward the island and started the motor.

The little island he had stared at through the mist from his hotel balcony three hours before now lay straight ahead, growing bigger and more intriguing every second. He searched the barren shore for a face, but no human was in sight. The motor stopped and they drifted in, letting the tiny waves push them toward the dark sandy beach. The fisherman jumped out and turned the boat sideways into the soft shell-covered shore.

Quickly taking his shoes off and clutching them to his chest, Paul turned to say thanks. Before he could utter a word, the boatman pulled the cord and the motor roared. He gave the boat a push toward the sea and waved good-bye. Soon he was out of sight.

Paul waded in toward the beach, stumbling over broken pieces of coral and seashells, his toes getting caught in moss-colored weeds and remnants of brown, feathery sponges. His eyes spanned the empty beach, as he tried to spot anyone looking for him. Seeing no one, he moved closer and tried to penetrate the depths of bramble to detect any movement. Suddenly his eye caught a quick grey spot darting to the left. He froze and clutched the revolver in his pants pocket. The bleat of a goat pierced his ear and he relaxed, seeing the animal emerge and gently make its way down the slope. Deciding to follow the shore, he walked along, allowing the waves to lap at his feet while his toes sank into the cool, soft mud. The relentless sun followed him, warming his back and neck. He turned his shirt collar up to protect his neck, wondering why he had bothered to heed this note. Maybe it was a joke. Why hadn't the fisherman told him his name? Why had he left so abruptly? But then he reminded himself that those in his profession always followed a lead, however odd and wherever it may take them.

He rounded a bend, and there in a sheltered cove lay a rotting boat hull and some fishing nets drying out from the morning's effort. Further on, some homemade wooden traps decorated the sand. He bent down to examine one, opening and closing the hinged door and turning it over. A tiny shadow was suddenly cast before him and he spun around to see a boy motioning him to follow. Paul left the beach and they grasped knotted roots and thick vines to pull themselves up onto the slopes above the beach. The ground became more solid and the little path travelled upward, the weeds and tall grasses giving way to thick overgrown bushes and small trees. Dark green leaves of exotic plants invaded their footpath and the sun broke through in spots to illuminate red-orange flowers. All at once the path opened to a clearing and he could almost feel the cool splash of a splendid waterfall, which cascaded down the lush, green stairway of fern-covered rock.

Paul stood nearly motionless as the boy disappeared behind a small grove of bushes. He wondered where the boy had gone as his eyes swept the untouched beauty of this island paradise. Tiny yellow birds sang sweet, high-pitched melodies and delicate orange hibiscus blossoms blended with the golden rays of the afternoon sun, bathing the clearing with a bright warm glow.

His sensitively trained ear heard the rustling of leaves and he spotted his guide. Behind him, holding the boy's hand and blinking into the piercing sunlight, was a tall, shapely, exquisitely tanned woman, her long black hair almost reaching her slender waist. Her white parea was wound tightly and sensuously around her, wrapping her full breasts and generous hips into one beautiful package. She slowly and gracefully glided past fragrant tropical bushes toward him, as if stepping out of a travel brochure. He was stunned. Was this the person who had written the note?

She stopped and without saying a word, beckoned for him to come nearer by lifting her head just a bit and turning it to the left. As he got closer, he could see her sparkling ink-black eyes above high cheekbones, while her full, fuchsia-colored lips were on the verge of creating just the hint of a smile at each edge of her mouth. A golden miniature sun disk hung on a delicate chain at her throat, and each of her wrists was adorned with several bangle bracelets. On her left

11

hand, in addition to a bracelet watch, was a thick, gold wedding band next to a large, emerald-cut diamond. The right hand sported a gold ring imbedded with two emeralds.

As Paul approached her, wanting to fold her into his arms but knowing he must be cautious, she tossed her head back, pushing her long, thick swatch of course hair aside and planting her bronzed legs firmly in front of her. Her lips parted and he heard a decidedly Spanish accent mingled with another foreign dialect he couldn't identify.

"So I see my uncle found you. I hope the ride was pleasant."

"The fisherman is your uncle?" he asked incredulously.

"Yes, he brought me here yesterday. This is my younger brother Tomás."

He glanced at the boy and shook his hand.

"Paul Brennan," he announced and turned to the woman as a way of introducing himself.

"I shall call you Paolo," she said dreamily. "It sounds more romantic in Italian."

The formality of this strange encounter began to make him nervous. He wanted to know *why* he had been brought to the island and he wanted to know *right away*.

"Why did you bring me here? What is your interest in me?" he questioned abruptly.

"Come, it is hot here in the sun. Let us walk under the cliff toward the waterfall pool," she suggested, pointing upward and grasping his hand, then gently pulling him along as she walked ahead. "I need your help to take a message to someone," she whispered, clutching his arm. "It is very important for me, for my father, and for my poor country."

"What is your poor country, if I might ask?" he questioned a bit sarcastically.

"I am Peruvian, although I have not lived there in awhile. I long to see my family, but I cannot return just now..." Her voice trailed off as they neared the pool of turquoise water. She ran to the edge and leaned over, her hair falling forward, creating a black curtain to hide her face. She cupped the cool, clear liquid to her lips and splashed her forehead. Then she turned to see Paul kneeling beside her. He stared down into the water, entranced by her reflection in the pool in front of them. Her cool, wet hand caressed his burning neck, and he pulled her hands away from him.

"Exactly what do you want me to do?" he demanded. "And why did you choose an American journalist for the job?"

"I told my uncle to find someone who could easily get into Cuba. He spotted you at the hotel two days ago when you arrived."

"Americans are not welcome in Cuba," he declared. Her delicate smile reappeared.

"Well, can't some Americans get permission? Perhaps those with family there, government officials, researchers, and journalists? You are a journalist, no?"

"I would need to get clearance from my government. I don't think I qualify. I have no reason to go there."

"But couldn't you invent a reason? You have government connections, don't you?" she asked slyly.

"Look, why should I risk my life and my career for you? And why go to Cuba? You said you were from Peru."

"My father is in Cuba. He is old and not well. I must let him know that I am alive and will return to him soon."

"Why can't your uncle take the message to him?"

"Sometimes it is better to trust a stranger," she answered in a sad, wistful tone. "No one from my family can go back right now. It is not safe. We must wait. You see, I had to leave South America very quickly."

Paul hesitated and then stood up.

"I am sorry, but there are too many unanswered questions for me to give you the answer you want me to give you. I need more information from you."

She looked downcast again, and lowered her head, turning it away from him.

"I do not want to put your life in danger. I cannot tell you everything," she murmured. Her eyes began to fill with tears as she slowly raised herself from the moist ground. Paul began to pace trying to think about her request. The words Peru, Cuba, and message ran through his mind. What did all of this mean?

Suddenly Tomás appeared with a basket of fruit and some wine.

"Sit down and eat," the woman purred, and Paul dutifully obeyed, not having had lunch. He bit into a large, ripe, red-orange nectarine and swallowed mouthfuls of cool white wine. He began to relax. Gazing into her deep dark eyes, he tried to discern the truth.

"I don't even know your name," he said in a half whisper. "Tell me about yourself."

"My name is Gabriella Rojas. I grew up on a coffee plantation in the Huallaga Valley of Peru. Do you know where that is?"

"Near the Amazon, I think," he murmured, while reaching for a banana.

"My father insisted that I go to school in the city, and when I was fourteen I went to Lima to live with my aunt and uncle so I could attend a good school. I was separated from my family for many months. When my mother died, I did not find out in time to attend the funeral. After I finished what you call high school, I returned to help Father on the ranch. But he didn't approve. He had promised my mother that I would have a better life than she had. They wanted me to study and become someone important. That summer, when I returned from Lima, I spent many days thinking. I would wander the hills wondering what to do with my young life. Then I met Carlos, and my world suddenly changed."

"Who is Carlos?"

"He is the oldest son of a very wealthy and influential family in Colombia. He has travelled with his father to Venezuela, Brazil, Miami, and Spain, and spent hours telling me of these adventures. He learned to be independent at a young age, and I was somehow drawn to his determination and ambition. I met his family and my father promised me to Carlos in exchange for helping me get a university education and introduction into proper social circles. Carlos's father paid for me to study so that one day I would be able to marry his son and be the kind of wife he deserved."

"Most American women would be angry to be told they weren't good enough to marry someone's son. Doesn't it bother you that this marriage was established as a deal in order to transform you into someone they wanted you to be?"

She raised her expressive, dark, flashing eyes.

"Many women have opportunities in America that I did not have. My father could never have afforded the cost of a private professional education and he did not have the right connections. It was an arrangement, yes, but I thought it was fair at the time. I not only received the chance for training and study, but I was also going to become the wife of a powerful and handsome man. Let's stop talking about Carlos, shall we? Tell me about yourself."

"Well, I grew up in a small family, in a small town in New Jersey. My father wanted me to be a lawyer, but I wasn't cut out for that, so I studied journalism in New York City. I love to travel and I enjoy meeting people and learning about other cultures. I work for a newspaper, and last year I was finally given international assignments. I recently spent some time reporting from Kashmir, and then Central Europe."

"Are you ever afraid to go to dangerous countries?"

"I think that danger can be found in any country. There is no safe haven. If we want to find out the truth, we need to take the risk and get as close as possible to people who can give us the answers. Of course I am afraid sometimes. But I have a job to do and have to use all my skills and knowledge to try and survive."

She stretched out on the grass and sipped her wine. "Yes, we all have to do that. Life is one long struggle to survive, especially in my country."

Paul leaned back on his elbow. "Where is Carlos now?"

"He is in Cuba, working with my father."

"What kind of work are they doing?"

"They are trying to improve the conditions for farmers like my father."

"Cuba? Why is your father there?"

She suddenly lowered her head and looked away. "He was forced to leave his country. That is all I can say."

Paul was touched by her story and inexplicably drawn to her. He moved closer to her, stretching out his arm so that he could cradle her head on his shoulder. A warm, tender feeling quickly surged over him, and he gently kissed her. She sat up abruptly.

"I must tell you that I am married to Carlos and need your help to get my message to Cuba. Will you help me?"

Paul looked into her hopeful face, her smile radiating warmth and honesty. He slowly stood up, offering his hand to help her.

"*If* I can get into Cuba, I will take your message. On two conditions: that you tell me everything you know about the work Carlos is involved in and that you meet me when I return."

She looked up into his eyes.

"Yes, of course," she murmured. "I will tell you as much as I know, but not enough to put your life in danger. When you return, meet me in Puerto Rico. My uncle will take you to me."

They finished the food and walked along the path, looking for Tomás while she told him small details about Carlos's family but nothing more about her father. He decided not to press her for more information when they saw Tomás coming toward them.

"My little brother will take you to the other side of the island where the tides are more favorable for my uncle to pick you up." She pushed a small brown envelope into his shirt pocket, and took his face in her hands.

"*Vaya con Dios*," she whispered in his ear, and as she kissed him he gathered her long dark hair between his hands. She pulled away and gave some directions to Tomás. They started off, and as Paul turned to wave good-bye to her, he could see her shading her eyes from the sun. She looked up to the blue skies and crossed herself, trying to safeguard his journey.

CHAPTER 2

Paul deftly dialed the number for the overseas desk at the newspaper in New York City, his mind swirling with thoughts while he waited to be connected.

"Dave? Paul. I'm still in St. Thomas, but I need a favor."

"Are you working already? I thought you were recuperating from that last assignment in Romania."

"I've had enough sun and sand and I'm getting restless. I need to get into Cuba to do a piece on their reaction to East European events. I met someone who tells me it's a real hot issue over there. Can you get me clearance?"

"Well, I don't know. It's almost impossible to get reporters into the country, even for a critical emergency story or one that would favor their political stand. On the other hand, it might be a good tie-in with Mike's work on the Miami connection to drug shipments. I'll see what I can do. It'll take a few days, though."

"I don't have a few days, Dave. Call me as soon as you get clearance. Fax me any necessary paperwork. Before you hang up, transfer me to Research."

While Paul waited, he thought of Gabriella and something she had said that stuck in his mind and just didn't sound right.

"Research? This is Paul Brennan. I need you to dig up some info on two families for me. One in Peru named Santiago. The other family is in Colombia...Rojas. Father Jorge, son Carlos...in the export business...coffee, hemp...yes, I know Santiago is a common name. I don't know much. Father is in exile in Cuba. The mother died years ago. There is a brother in Lima named José. The father owns or works a coffee plantation in the Huallaga Valley. What? No, I can't be more specific about location. Wait! This is important. He has a daughter Gabriella who studied in Lima and went to the National University in Bogotá. She had to leave the country suddenly. I need to know why she left. ASAP. Thanks. I'm staying at the Virgin Isle Hotel. Hello?"

The connection suddenly sounded muffled. He yelled into the receiver

"Dave at the international desk upstairs can give you all the contact information for me. Can you hear me?" The line went dead.

He hung up, and then dialed special operations at the State Department.

"Hello, this is 2791. I need to speak to Brian Matthews on a secure line."

"Type in the code word and when we have set up the call, we will ring twice. Answer with the normal response."

Paul tapped the code and hung up. He lit a cigarette. How was he going to talk State into helping him get into Cuba? Would Brian believe his story? He couldn't tell him that a voluptuous Peruvian beauty enticed him into agreeing to take a message there. He had to use his job as a cover. He closed his eyes, but all he saw was Gabriella looking up at the sky. Her voice drifted back to him. He slipped out of his loafers and socks, and looked out of the window. The phone rang twice, then stopped. He waited. It rang again and he put out the cigarette and grabbed the receiver.

"Hello, this is Brennan 2791."

"Brian Matthews speaking."

"Brian, how are you?"

"Tired and ready to retire! How can I help you?"

"I've been assigned to cover a story in Cuba and I need a contact there. Someone with low visibility."

"You'll need my help to get into Cuba. How long will you be there?"

"I'm not sure. I need to do a lot of interviewing of both government officials and citizens, and as you know, that can be difficult to arrange quickly."

"Neil Taylor is in Havana now, but he may have to leave any day. I can't be sure. When are you leaving?"

"As soon as I can get permission. Can you help speed that along, by the way?"

"I'll try to do what I can, but things take time, even here in the US. I think I might have someone willing to shadow you. Antonio Cenera. As low-key as they come. He blends in like a native. Code name is Mango. I think he was born in Lima."

"How long has he been with State?"

"I'm not exactly sure, but I can check. He just arrived in Havana yesterday to look into a situation that is heating up down there. He'll be at the Morocco, room 714. I'll alert him and have him contact you once you arrive."

"Thanks, Brian. What is he investigating?"

"We're not sure if it is a problem, but the boys at the Pentagon don't want to take any chances. They've intercepted some chatter from the Cuban government that points to a possible interest in South American affairs. I can't say any more than that. Security, you know."

"I understand. I'll call you after I meet Mango."

Paul hung up and leaned back on his pillow, lighting another cigarette. He began to ask himself some questions to sort it all out. Did Gabriella believe in what Carlos was doing? Why was he to meet her in Puerto Rico? What connection did Cuba have with Peru? Thoughts of Gabriella's face suddenly came back to him. Why can't she return? What is she afraid of? He began to drift off when a knock at the door jarred him awake. Getting up, he opened the door. There was no one around. Clotilde was not in sight. As he closed the door, he felt something rough with his left foot. Looking down he noticed a white business card on the rug. He bent down and scooped it up. The card advertised a well-known jewelry store downtown. On the back, an awkwardly scrawled note read: Leave Thursday, 5 p.m. Airport. Will contact you. We meet in Havana. Uncle.

Downstairs in the dining room, he finished his Campari and tasted his gazpacho. Sometimes he wished his only job was that of a newspaper correspondent and not someone with ties to the State Department. He wondered what Mango looked like. It would be nice to have a trustworthy contact in Cuba. Was he really wise getting involved with this woman and her family? He hated to lie to Brian, but then again it might lead to a fantastic story for the paper. The band suddenly stopped playing to take a break. His grilled mahimahi dinner was placed on the table and he sipped his cool Chablis, beginning to relax in the quieter atmosphere. Thoughts of Gabriella came drifting back to soothe him. He wondered what she was doing now. Questions and doubts began to dog him again. What if he got in too deep and angered the paper? He thought about a colleague who had pushed too far for a lead and was moved to a small domestic paper and finally fired. The more delicate position was the one at State, which could have more important consequences if things went wrong in Cuba. He would hate to cause harm to his country and his family.

A native floor show started and he slowly became absorbed in the dancing. Bright orange torches seemed to cast a glow that mesmerized him, reminding him of the golden sun overhead on French cap. One of the dancers suddenly appeared at his table, her long black hair just grazing his arm. It reminded him of Gabriella as she waved good-bye to him that afternoon. Shaking his head no as the woman tried to pull him onto the dance floor, she took the hint and glided over to another male seated alone. The joyful look on the man's face indicated that she had been successful.

As the man got up to dance, Paul saw that he was tall and middle-aged with a noticeable bald spot. Three lovely island beauties encircled the man and began to spin him. All at once the male dancer's attention drifted away from the girls and glanced in Paul's direction. Suddenly the music stopped and the girls retired, leaving the man alone on the dance floor. He started to walk toward Paul's table and Paul searched his memory for a name or place that would connect the man to his past. Just then, the waitress appeared with his bill.

"You have a phone call, Mr. Brennan. Do you want to come to the reservation area to take it?"

"No, transfer it to my room," he said as he got up and pulled some bills from his wallet. When he turned back, the dance floor was empty and the bald man had vanished.

About to shove the key into the lock of his door, he stopped, hearing a sound coming from inside the room. Was someone inside? Was Clotilde turning the bed down and leaving chocolate? No lights were on. The sound stopped. He quickly opened the door and thought he noticed movement on the balcony. Running through the room, he quickly pushed the sliding glass door open. No one was there. He looked below at the swimming pool where noisy teens were splashing and laughing. No one else seemed to be around. Re-entering the room, he picked up the phone but got a dial tone. He dialed the front desk.

"This is Paul Brennan. Was a call transferred to room 518? It came through when I was in the restaurant."

"I'm sorry, but that call was transferred and then the caller hung up."

Paul replaced the receiver and switched on the lamp. The fax machine lights were blinking. That must have been the sound he heard. Glossy paper sat in the bin. He picked it up and saw the name of his paper at the top edge:

Clearance for assignment Cuba approved. One week only. Send us reports. Overseas Desk.

Paul slipped his shoes off and removed his jacket, hanging it on the back of a chair. He locked the door before turning off the light. Closing his eyes, he began drifting off to sleep, seeing shadows of native dancers and Gabriella. He imagined her voice gently speaking to him, soothing and comforting him as they floated along in a canoe on a lake. The repeated buzz of the phone jarred him awake and erased all hopes of a reunion. His dream was gone.

"Hello," he yelled into the receiver, switching on the lamp and looking at the clock which blinked 1:15 a.m. to him in red numbers. A soft mellow voice travelled to his ear.

"I miss you, Paolo. Did you receive my uncle's message?"

His dream of hearing her voice suddenly became real, but instead of letting him relax, her words made him feel uneasy.

"Gabriella, are you all right?"

"Yes, my darling. I am fine."

"I got your uncle's message. I already have the go-ahead from the newspaper, but I still need to wait to hear from the State Department."

"I am sure you will get permission" she said softly. "But Paolo, be careful. I think someone else might be watching you."

"Who?"

"I don't know. Perhaps the men who made my father leave do not want you to take my note to him."

"Is there anything more I should know that you didn't tell me?"

"No nothing," she half whispered.

"I promise to be careful, Gaby. Now go to sleep and dream of us." He didn't mention the possible intruder or the man in the restaurant, and marveled at the way he wanted to protect this woman he hardly knew.

"*Vaya con Dios*, my love" she murmured quietly and he heard the click of the phone.

He turned off the light and closed his eyes but couldn't sleep. Something she said about her father clung to his mind and wouldn't let go. Why had some men forced him to leave his home? What had happened? Why wouldn't they want him to take the note to her father? The note! He had forgotten. Where had he put it? Should he open it? These thoughts began to drift through his brain when sleep overtook him. The note would have to wait until tomorrow.

CHAPTER 3

Carlos stretched his tanned, muscular arm across the cream-colored satin sheets toward the night table. His hand groped for his gold watch. He grabbed it and dangled it above his head, trying to see the time. A slender, feminine arm reached up from under the sheets and slipped the watch from his grip. She held it by her pink-polished fingertips and said sleepily

"It is 9:15. Your father will be here soon."

"Leave the house and do not come back here this week. I will be busy in Havana with my father." Carlos threw the covers back and walked to the window. He lit a cigarette and looked out over the long circular driveway and the huge iron fence beyond the hedges. His companion stood up, tossed the watch on her pillow, and disappeared into the bathroom to take a shower. Carlos put his cigarette out and began to dress. He surveyed himself in the large, gold-edged, full-length mirror. His shiny black curls framed a somewhat boyish face, but his solid build and strong arms reflected a mature masculinity. His unbuttoned shirt revealed a chest of curly black hair and a gold chain attached to a cross hung from his neck. His striking blue eyes contrasted with his dark hair and skin, arresting in a charming sort of way. He picked up the phone and dialed.

"Is my father here yet? Good. I'll be right down." He looked out the window and saw the limo with the huge gold "J R" engraved on the side of the door and on the roof of the car. Just then, the woman came out of the bathroom and walked over to him. She leaned into his body from behind. Wrapping her arms around his waist, she began to kiss his neck. He quickly grabbed her arms and twisted her around, shoving her away with his knee.

"I said I didn't want to see you for awhile! I will call you later. Get dressed quickly!" Then he caught her neck in his huge, powerful hands and pressed her face toward his own, kissing her forcefully and then pushing her aside and walking out of the bedroom.

Father and son met at the bottom of the stairs in a warm embrace. It was clear that there was a strong, close bond between them. They were not only father and son, but business partners and confidants.

"Father, are you well?"

"Yes, of course," the elder Rojas replied. "I am looking forward to our discussions with the Cuban officials, and I am very proud and honored to have my eldest son at my side. You are a great asset to me, Carlos. Someday the business will be yours and I know you will be a success at it."

"Sometimes I am not so sure of that, Father. Gabriella's family doesn't seem to think..."

"Forget about her family. They may change their minds if we accomplish our mission today and continue to be successful."

The maid handed Carlos his briefcase and opened the front door. Jorge Rojas gently squeezed her arm and whispered something to her as he walked out of the house.

****

Rain fell softly outside and no sunlight penetrated the drapes of the balcony window. Dark clouds hung above the palms, which swayed from the ever-increasing northern winds. Paul suddenly became aware of a green light and then a whirring sound. Of course, the fax was on and transmitting! Dave must be up early...or was it late? Looking at the clock and seeing the red digital numbers 8:05 a.m., he pulled the sheets over his head and turned over. This day will be long enough, he thought. Why get up now?

As he started to close his eyes, he suddenly remembered his last thought before falling asleep the night before: Gaby's note! He had to get up and find it. Sprinting out of bed, he started combing through his jacket pockets. What was he wearing last night? Then he spotted the edge of a brown envelope sticking out of the pocket of his green Izod shirt. Carefully pulling it out, he turned it over. Gabriella had written her father's name on the outside: Ricardo Santiago. Paul hadn't thought to look at the envelope before he called Research. Now he began to remember details…. Rosa was her mother's name. Fingering the envelope, he noticed that it was thicker than he had remembered. It was also sealed. He guessed that Gaby wasn't as trusting as he had imagined. Should he steam it open? He never promised not to read it. Hunger pangs began to strike and he threw it down on the chair and called room service for breakfast. Then he showered and turned on the TV. He casually glanced at the fax messages: a formal letter from the paper sending him to Cuba for a story and a list of officials he could contact. That was all.

He opened the drapes and looked out. Heavy mist obscured French cap and the bay was empty of ships. Rain drops splattered the windowpanes and the trees swayed back and forth in the strong wind.

The smell of hot coffee told him that breakfast was near, and he opened the door for the cart to be wheeled into the room. As he buttered a roll he listened to the news and tried to catch up on global reporting. Kashmir was a hotbed of violence and he thought of an old friend who would be covering the events. He missed working with her. They had parted in Romania when she was sent to India, and he had decided to come home for awhile to try and report on something less demanding and dangerous. Now he wished he had stayed, or gone to India with Allison. He didn't particularly want to go to Cuba, especially not knowing exactly why he was going there. This whole business felt strange and made him uneasy. Perhaps he should call it off.

The phone rang and he answered.

"Paul Brennan? This is the research department of *World News*. We have the information that you requested."

Reaching for a pencil and paper, he said "Go ahead."

"Ricardo Santiago is sixty-six years old. Widower. He no longer owns his own ranch. About three years ago he sold it to pay off debts. We're not sure who owns it, but every month he used to get a visit from one of the Rojas sons. Mr. Santiago apparently married above his class and neighbors say he is poor but happy and loves his family very much. Jorge Rojas, on the other hand, is very powerful and wealthy. Has three sons and one daughter. He is extremely close to the oldest, Carlos, who accompanies him on trips and is groomed to take over someday. Other sons Eduardo and Gualberto help in the business but are not included in high-level decision making. His business is somewhat mysterious. He has holdings in coffee and Venezuelan oil and also seems to be politically connected. He and Carlos travel a great deal. The company they keep is interesting. Older wealthy landowners as well as the younger "new money" set. They have been guests of politicians and aristocrats and have been seen in barrio brothels. The two of them are great womanizers."

"What about the Santiago daughter?"

"Gabriella Maria Rosa Santiago was born in Peru in 1963. She graduated with a degree in economics from the university in Bogotá in 1986. She was politically active during that time. Her picture appeared more than once in the newspaper. She married Carlos Rojas in 1987 at a big wedding with lots of political big shots attending. Her activism abruptly ceased. Couple honeymooned in Spain at her father-in-law's private villa and returned to occupy a large estate outside Bogotá. Carlos owns a summer house about forty miles outside of San Juan, Puerto Rico as well as other properties in Venezuela and Peru."

"But what about the girl's disappearance?"

"We couldn't get much on that but we're still working on it. Apparently there had been some disagreement between the two families over the business. According to our investigator, the girl's older brother was killed by a car bomb when things turned ugly. The father and daughter fled with the help of her uncle who exports orchids and owns a farm. We think they may have been coerced into leaving. That's all I have but I'll contact you in a few days."

"Thanks. I may be in Havana by then."

"We'll track you down. Keep paper in your fax and check your computer. We're sending you this material…clippings, transcriptions of interviews, reports."

"Thanks again. I am sure it will be helpful." He hung up and returned to his breakfast.

He began to write down some notes before he forgot the details. He still didn't know much about the Rojas's business but was getting a clearer picture of the players: a strong family with lots of political connections who travelled a lot. Why the trips? Was it a legitimate business? What was the disagreement about? Property? He began to surmise that Rojas may have forced Santiago to sign his ranch over to him and then pressured him to leave the country. But where did the son fit in? Who killed him and why? Did Rojas order it?

He got up and went out on the balcony. The storm was over and the clouds were slowly moving away. Everything was moist and the air was warm and humid. He still didn't know if he could go to Cuba tomorrow. He returned to the room and dialed Washington but couldn't get through. He needed to walk. Leaving the hotel, he began to follow the road to town. Trucks full of sugarcane field workers passed him. He stopped at a small grocery store and bought some bread and fruit. While watching the boats in the harbor, he peeled a banana, wondering if he would be sleeping in Havana soon.

CHAPTER 4

Jorge Rojas nervously paced back and forth in the anteroom of the diplomat's chambers, wondering why his son was taking so long. Carlos only needed to sign a few forms to get permission to see the general. He passed a huge, gold-framed mirror and stopped in front of it to admire himself. He liked what he saw: silver-grey temples and sparkling eyes stared back at him. He smiled, and then walked to the huge, high window. His tall imposing figure looked down at the wide boulevard and he watched the cars pass: large old American monstrosities chugging along, struggling to function properly on worn parts and rebuilt motors. It made one nostalgic for the past, Rojas thought, as he pulled a Cuban cigar from the blue, silk-lined pocket of his Italian-made suit. He lit it, and puffed smoke against the windowpane, which coated the glass with a cloudy, brown-tinged film.

This sixty-year-old patriarch lent a distinguished air to the gloomy waiting room. Here was someone who had obviously been tutored at home as a boy, had played polo, drank fine wines and used smart tailors in the best cities. The outer door suddenly opened and a young typist entered the room, her arms full of huge, heavy ledgers.

"Let me assist you, my dear," Rojas insisted, hurrying to move closer and taking the large books from her aching arms.

"Oh thank you, sir," she said as she gladly surrendered them to his strong hands, looking up to see his cold, steel-grey eyes that seemed to penetrate her soul. She knocked on the inner door of the secretary's office and went in. Rojas did not see anyone inside for the brief instant that the door was open. He placed the books on the desk and began to pace again. Soon she returned with the forms that Carlos had signed.

"They won't be long, sir. Then you both will be driven to the general's headquarters."

"Thank you, dear lady. You are so kind to let me know. We are anxious to finish our business and get back to Colombia. Have you ever been there?"

"No sir, I haven't. My mother has a cousin who lives in Cartagena, but we never found the opportunity to travel."

"I know Cartagena well," declared Rojas, moving closer to the young typist who was now sitting behind her desk. "It is a beautiful port city with much activity. You must visit your relative some day. I can arrange a trip if you like." He leaned across the desk and stared into her eyes, his jacket brushing her arm.

The typist squirmed uncomfortably. "My fiancé and I are saving our money for a wedding trip to Rio. I have dreamed of going there since I was a child."

"Will your government permit such travel?" Rojas asked with some agitation.

Just then, Carlos opened the door and came out with the secretary.

"All is done, Father. We must go now. The driver is waiting for us downstairs to take us to headquarters."

The elder Rojas shrugged his shoulders. Taking the typist's hand, he brushed it lightly with his lips and bid her farewell. The two men walked briskly down the marble staircase and out the front door to the military car.

****

Gabriella sat at the kitchen table and stared down at the plate of spareribs and spicy peppers that Anna had prepared for her lunch. This was her favorite Peruvian dish, but today she had no appetite. She got up and walked to the huge window and looked out beyond the gravel path toward the road. She could almost hear the gentle ocean waves meeting the sandy beach behind and down the embankment from the great house. Why had Carlos insisted on her coming back to their estate in Puerto Rico so soon? Did he resent her enjoying herself in St. Thomas, or did he just want to enjoy his mistress in Bogotá without his wife around? Suddenly she saw Anna waving from the path on her way in to the house. Gabriella waved back and tried to smile. She quickly returned to the table, not wanting her loyal cook and confidante to think she didn't appreciate the meal that was so lovingly prepared for her. Picking up a fork, she began to play with the food, pretending to eat. Anna was the one who named her Gaby and spent hours on the beach taking care of her, playing children's games, looking for shells, or explaining why the moon changes its shape. Gabriella missed her when she went to school and then moved away, and Anna comforted her when her mother and brother died and tried to help her adjust to married life with Carlos.

Anna opened the door and hung her jacket on the hook next to the window.

She quickly noticed that Gaby had hardly touched the full plate of food, and stood behind her, pulling Gaby's long dark hair back and away from her face, letting it trail down her back. She rubbed Gaby's shoulders and kissed the top of her head.

"What is wrong? You have not touched your food!"

"I am sorry, Anna. I cannot eat right now. I am too sad." She put the fork down and lowered her head.

Anna looked into her eyes and sat down next to her.

"What is making you so sad, my little angel?"

"I keep thinking of how sad my life really is. My father is angry with me and won't speak to me, and I miss Roberto so much! Carlos is moody and difficult. I know he has a mistress in Bogotá. That is probably why he didn't want me to return to our house there and instead sent me here."

"Tell me about St. Thomas. I have never been there. Didn't you have a nice time on the island?"

Gabriella looked up and suddenly smiled. She picked up her fork again and began to eat.

"Yes, Anna, I was happy there. The beaches and sunsets are wonderful and the food is very good, although it can't compare to your paella! And it was nice to spend some time with Tomás. He is getting so big now!"

"Did you do anything else besides swimming and eating?"

Gaby put down her fork and glanced sideways at Anna. Her eyes had regained that sparkle, and her lips curved up at the edges, revealing a sly smile.

"Yes, I did. I met a journalist from the US. His name is Paul Brennan. We had a long talk and he is going to help take a message to Father."

"That is good news! You must eat now and think only of a happy reunion with your dear father. When you are finished why don't you take a walk on the beach? That always helped you relax when you were young."

"All right. But only if you start calling my father Ricardo! You have known him for so many years. You are part of the family, Anna!"

"Yes, but I am also a servant who knows her place. I don't think your husband would approve."

"Carlos doesn't own you, Anna, and he doesn't own me! I will speak to him when he arrives and persuade Father to talk to him about it."

Gabriella tasted the peppers and her appetite suddenly seemed to improve. She happily chewed the ribs, then wiped her hands on the soft cotton napkin and finished the sangria. She opened the door and walked to the back of the house. Running down the sloped embankment to the beach, she breathed in the fresh air and dipped her toes into the ocean. She looked up at the blue sky and spoke Paolo's name, whispering her good luck mantra to him while she crossed herself. She hoped to be reunited soon with her father, but she wanted to see Paolo even more.

■■■

The Rojas men stepped out of the car and onto the driveway which led to an old Spanish mission. They were greeted by several armed guards who frisked them and then motioned with their

Kalashnikovs to move toward the church. The bell began to chime as they followed the men into the damp, dimly lit sanctuary which was now being used to house military officials. General Rodriguez opened the door of a tiny room off the chapel at the back of the church.

"Jorge, how nice to see you! So this is the son I've heard so much about!"

"Bernardo, it has been too long." The two old comrades embraced each other and sat down.

"This is my oldest son Carlos. Carlos, you have heard me talk of my close friend Bernardo Rodriguez. You finally meet him,"

"Carlos, you look like your father did thirty years ago when we worked together in these hills, but even more sophisticated."

"It is a pleasure to meet you, General Rodriguez."

"The younger generation is interested not only in wealth but in living well and enjoying the fruits of their labors. You know, Bernardo, when we were young we were more idealistic."

The men all squeezed into the small room. The general slipped behind his huge oak desk while the other two sat down on wicker-seated chairs obviously taken from the church.

Opening a box of cigars, Bernardo held it out to each man. Jorge eagerly removed one while Carlos waved it off.

"And what are you interested in these days, Jorge?"

"What we were always interested in, Bernardo—Power...and to provide a good life for our children, of course."

"Ah, yes. You are fortunate to have sons, Jorge. I have four daughters and none of them took an interest in the military. I have many dowries to provide. What about you, Carlos? Ever thought of a career like mine?"

"I am told that I have a head for business, General. I enjoy travelling and dealing with people in the civilian world. My father has told me about the challenges you were both faced with when you were young. I don't think I would have wanted to sacrifice so much of my personal life for political causes."

"Perhaps you would have thought differently had you grown up with us, Carlos. But now, how can I be of service to you as businessmen and to your country?"

Carlos's father cleared his throat. "The plan we spoke of on the phone last month could benefit Cuba and Colombia at the same time. It involves a trade of sorts. Cuba provides a service to our brave Colombian men and it receives generous payment for it. Your job is to sell it to your government; I have already paved the way with officials at home and they are quite supportive."

Jorge Rojas leaned back in his chair and proceeded to discuss details with his old friend. Carlos listened intently, trying to learn as much as he could about his father's method of persuasion. Perhaps someday he would be planning the strategies. Right now he was just taking notes. While timetables and logistics were being established, Carlos looked out of the tiny window behind the general's desk. Someone was hurrying toward the church. Soon a loud knock interrupted the conversation, and the door opened.

"General Rodriguez, I am sorry to interrupt, but you must come at once to the radio room. There is an urgent message for you from town."

"You will have to excuse me, gentlemen. I will begin to work on this project immediately."

"Thank you, Bernardo. I am confident that you will be successful. It will mean a great deal for our poor farmers and will provide Cuba with a lucrative commodity."

"I will be in touch very soon, Jorge. Have a good trip back." They quickly clasped hands and the general departed. Father and son then climbed into a car and were driven back to town for lunch.

CHAPTER 5

Stepping out of the cab, Paul carried his luggage into the dilapidated hotel lobby. Seeing the desk crowded with people, he dropped down into a dusty, worn armchair, sniffing the warm, stale air which smelled like a mixture of rum and recent cigar ash. He lifted his legs onto a scratched, 1950s-style coffee table in front of the chair, and picked up a torn copy of yesterday's newspaper which was on the floor under the small table. He stared at the photo of Castro at some kind of outdoor celebration and tried to read the caption. Looking up, he noticed that the reception desk clerk was alone, so he stood up and went over to get his room key.

He climbed the creaky stairs and walked down the dimly lit hallway. Finding his room, he unlocked the door and pushed it open. Pieces of green paint that had peeled off the walls coated the floor, and there was no window. The single, narrow, iron bed was covered with a thin, worn, yellow-green quilt decorated with palm trees. The blond wooden night stand was covered with a dusty film, except for the spot that the phone occupied. A small lamp with a rust-colored burn hole in the shade had a cracked base, exposing a frayed wire leading down to the floor's only electrical outlet, also covered in a greasy film. Turning around to investigate the bathroom, he saw dead roaches and water bugs littering the cracked tiles around the sink. He tried the faucet and a sickly brown liquid trickled out of the tap. *Maybe the shower at the end of the hall is in better shape*, he thought, as he began to unpack, plugging the fax adapter into the dusty receptacle he had seen behind the bed.

After showering, he decided to take a stroll down to the Malecón. The wide boulevard next to the ocean always reminded him of the afternoon he had spent talking to his father about adolescent mysteries. Havana had been different then, when his family came here on vacation. He and his sister had roamed the old city streets in search of treasures and swam in the warm Caribbean currents. At night, they listened to the street sounds from their hotel beds while their parents enjoyed the nightlife. They were denied the adult pleasures of dancing to Cuban bands, seeing glamorous floor shows, and participating in the casino activity which was deemed inappropriate for their age. Perhaps now he would get his chance, he mused.

Crossing the street, he hurried along, trying to remember which alley led down to the water. It was just dusk and the lights from the hotels along the oceanfront were turning on, helping him find his way. He smelled the fishy, salty odor of the sea and breathed it in, almost running to try to regain his youth by reliving the innocent past—when his parents were still alive. He spotted the sea wall just across the next street, and he could hear the waves breaking onto the jetties. The high stone wall bordered the road, and he walked along, following the curve of the land, peering out into the darkening depths of the Caribbean Sea. Lighting a cigarette, he paused and thought about how his grandfather had come here in the twenties to kick up his heels, and how twenty years later his father had spent his honeymoon here and later brought the family to witness prerevolutionary Cuba at the height of its popularity with American tourists.

The high-rise hotels and apartment houses which skirted the bay were just ahead. *What magnificent views they must have*, he thought. He stopped again and leaned over the wall trying to remember that cool evening walk he had taken with his dad. Where exactly along this wall had they stood and what had they discussed so fervently? He seemed to remember asking him subtle questions about girls and dating. *It must have been difficult for my father to give me advice on the anxiety I felt about approaching my teen years*, he thought. He suddenly felt a pang of sorrow that his father was not there to share the moment. It would have been nice to laugh together about it now.

Several women walked by and casually glanced at him. They said something in Spanish which he couldn't translate. Hearing the sound of that language made him think of Gabriella and why he was in Cuba. He lit another cigarette and started to walk back the way he came. An old '57 Chevy passed by, its motor laboring on bald tires with its exhaust pipe dragging on the ground. He turned to the ocean once more and tossed the butt on the ground, gazing at the half moon that had climbed higher into the black evening sky. Suddenly

36

someone caught his elbow and he wheeled around to see Gabriella's uncle, who led him away from the wall and down the street.

"You like Havana?"

"My room leaves a lot to be desired, but I suppose it was worth seeing this spot again. What are the plans?"

"Meet me tomorrow at ten in front of the National Theater. We go to see my brother at Varadero, not far from here."

"You mean her father isn't here in Havana?"

"No, for security reasons he is staying away from the city. But you will like Varadero. Bring your swimsuit. The beach is quite nice."

With that, he disappeared around a corner. Paul began to walk briskly toward what was once the luxury hotel area. He decided to try to find his contact. Hailing a taxi, he rode to the Morocco Hotel and went up to room 714. After knocking and getting no reply, he went down to the lobby and went to the desk.

"Excuse me. Do you know Mr. Cenera in room 714? Has he gone out?"

"Yes, he left twenty minutes ago. You want to leave a message?"

"Do you know where he went?"

The clerk hesitated. Paul pulled out a five dollar bill and slid it across the counter.

Shrugging off his reticence, the clerk's eyes brightened as he picked up the currency and shoved it into his pocket.

"I am sure he went to his favorite night spot. I'll call you a cab."

Paul jumped out of the taxi and pushed a ten dollar bill into the driver's hand, who grinned with pleasure while he looked into the rearview mirror to see if anyone was watching them. When he saw nothing unusual, he yelled a heavily accented thank you in English before slowly driving ahead, cruising for passengers. Paul entered the lobby which had seen better days. Russian and East European tourists congregated at different tables, buying bottles of island rum and cigars. Women in tight, slinky gowns emerged from the bathroom next to the stairs, chattering while they fought for a place at the large, cracked, fingerprinted mirror to admire themselves or add a touch of lipstick. Paul pushed past the group and climbed the stairs where he heard a loud marimba band blaring out rhumbas that his parents had surely danced to when they visited. Above the dance floor, on a separate platform, a bar beckoned, and he sprinted up the few steps and ordered a rum and Coke. He turned to survey the room. So this is what I had missed when I was thirteen, he thought.

Well-endowed showgirls wearing heavy, decorated headpieces slowly and sensuously sauntered back and forth on the stage. Their elaborate costumes dripped with colored sequins and rhinestones, and he marveled at how well they balanced and maneuvered in what resembled lampshades or chandeliers. They began to sing and dance, and toward the end of the song, the headdresses flickered and then lit up like Times Square on New Year's Eve.

He looked around trying to spot Mango, but not knowing what he looked like made it difficult. The bartender was nearby cleaning glasses.

"Excuse me, but do you know someone named Tonio Cenera?"

With a shake of his head to say no, he put the glass down. "Want another?"

"Sure." Paul threw down the price of two drinks and a generous tip, deciding to walk around a bit once he had the drink, to see if he could spot this contact who "blended in like a native" in Brian Matthews's words.

The first show ended and the band members stopped playing and began to put their instruments into the cases. In the opposite corner, an aging Polish pianist made the keys purr a bit before introducing his jazz quartet. A distinguished-looking black percussionist dressed in a white suit set the pace with brush and cymbal, his toe gently tapping out the beat. Another islander in African garb held the conga drum between his fat legs and tapped out Cuban rhythms, while a skinny, nervous saxophonist wailed sweet notes through palsied fingers, his head bobbing and shaking when he waited for his turn to play. His threadbare suit jacket sleeves revealed thin, arthritic wrists, and his garish orange tie hung down against a hollow, white-shirted chest, swinging back and forth with the movement of the sax. His part ended, and as he listened to the other three play, he pursed his lips and nodded his head. Focusing down on his well-worn shoes with his hands folded in front of him as if in prayer, he drowned himself in the music, feeling each rhythm through his wasted body. His red, swollen eyes and pallid skin revealed him to be a drug user, and he suddenly grasped the golden saxophone with both hands as if he needed it for support.

Paul weaved around the small round tables trying to notice single men who might be his contact. A Cuban girl selling cigars asked him to dance and he declined, saying he was looking for his wife. Suddenly a possibility was sighted at the back of the room and Paul wandered slowly to the little table in the corner. Standing behind the man who was seated, he quietly announced, "I think they are selling some fresh mangos in the lobby."

The reply was swift in a barely accented voice.

"Journalists shouldn't eat the local fruit." He pointed to the chair opposite and Paul sat down while he studied Mango's sparkling dark eyes and black, slicked-back hair pomaded with sickeningly sweet hair dressing. His broad shoulders gave him an air of authority even though he appeared to be rather short. Brian was right. He looked like a permanent Cuban resident instead of a US government agent.

"I'm Paul Brennan. Did Brian tell you why I was in Cuba?"

"He said something about delivering a message to a girl's father."

"That's right. I haven't met him yet, but her uncle plans to take me to see him tomorrow at Varadero."

"That's about an hour from Havana. Tell me more about this girl."

"She's Peruvian, married to a Colombian businessman by the name of Rojas. She tells me her father was exiled here, and he and the husband are working to improve life for Peruvian farmers."

Mango let out a derisive laugh, then became serious.

"The Rojas family has had its hands in many operations. Right now they are sympathetic to the drug lords. The father spends a lot of time in Cartagena, overseeing shipments."

"Drug shipments? Where are they going?"

"Probably to the US, first to drop-off points in the Caribbean; who knows where else? He covers his tracks with his business deals and travels a lot. In fact, you just missed him. He and his son were here in Havana this morning, according to my sources."

"Do you know what they were doing here?"

"I was told that they spent time talking to a general in the military. We are trying to find out what deal they are making but it most likely involves weapons."

"I don't know, Mango. I find it hard to believe she is involved in drug trafficking."

"She may not be. But don't be so naïve about the woman. She probably knows much more than she told you."

"I called the paper's research department so they could do some fact checking on names and information. But I've been reluctant to read the note she gave me to give to her father."

"Don't be stupid. Read it. She may be playing games with you. Listen. Be careful with Rojas. He has murdered people in the past."

A sudden chill went through him, and he reached into his coat pocket and withdrew the brown envelope. Hesitating, he slid it across the table to Mango.

"Open it."

Mango quickly picked up the candle that was in the center of the table and held it up near the flap, slowly moving it back and forth. Then, he took out a thin pocketknife and slid it carefully underneath the sealed edge. He cleanly separated the two sides and gingerly lifted out two sheets of pink paper. As he read, Paul detected the faint smell of Gaby's perfume. He searched Mango's face for some sign of concern, but saw no outward signs of emotion from his contact, who remained cool and quiet. At last he refolded the note and put it back into the envelope.

"When the waitress comes by, order a Cointreau. Rub a tiny bit across the flap to reseal it. The note was in Spanish. I'm not sure she is directly involved in her husband's business, but she asks her father forgiveness for her brother's death and wants him to meet Carlos to resolve their differences. She says something about understanding his side of things. She tells him she is safe and will see him in Puerto Rico on the twentieth. Oh yes, she also mentions her handsome messenger and tells the father to be careful what he says to you. "

"She told me that Carlos and her father were here in Havana working to help Peruvian farmers!"

"Apparently she lied to you. It seems like her father and Carlos are not speaking."

"She is as wary of me as I am of her. How can I get to know her better if we distrust each other so much?"

"Don't get emotional about all this, Brennan. I am warning you to be careful. Deliver the message and go back to the States. Forget that you ever met her."

"I can't do that. I told her I'd meet her in Puerto Rico after I delivered the message. And I want to see her again."

"Okay. She'll probably be at the summer house that Carlos owns. If you go there and notice anything that points to drug running, let me know. I'll be in Havana for a few more days. You know how to contact me." Mango got up and called a waitress over for Paul to order the drink. Before she got to the table, he leaned over Paul's shoulder and whispered, "See you on the beach. Under the tree. Red swim trunks." Then he walked out to the lobby and out the front door.

Paul ordered the drink. As he watched middle-aged Russians dance, he wondered if Gaby believed in what Carlos might be doing, and if she knew much about the "business," whatever it was. She seemed so innocent. Perhaps that was just an act to make him believe her so he'd deliver the note. The drink arrived and he took a few sips. He was becoming confused and scared. "What was I doing here?" he thought as he dipped his finger into the liquid and smeared a bit across the flap. As he pressed it down firmly to make it hold, someone brushed past the table coming off the dance floor. He looked up to see a tall man, his bald spot shining in the light from the disco ball overhead. Recognizing him as the person on the dance floor in St. Thomas, he shoved the envelope into his pocket and threw down a few dollars. He raced down the stairs and out to the lobby to follow him, wondering what he was doing here in Havana and whether he had followed him. The lobby tables were all empty now. He quickly checked the men's room. There was no sight of him. He pushed the front door open and looked left and right. There he was, walking up the street from the hotel, his arm around what looked like a prostitute. Paul ran a bit to catch up and followed behind them. They turned into a dark alley and began to go up a stairway. Suddenly he began to feel dizzy and everything around him darkened. The couple had vanished and he felt a push and fell to the ground.

CHAPTER 6

"Hey Brennan, wake up!" Paul heard Mango's voice as he slowly opened his eyes. He was still in the alley, sprawled on the ground.

"What happened?"

"I followed you out of the hotel and saw someone push you. Then a tall guy ran down the stairs and they both took off before I could get to you."

Paul rubbed his head. "I was following the tall guy. I had seen him in St. Thomas. Then I began to feel dizzy."

"Looks like someone might have spiked the Cointreau. I didn't tell you to drink it! Can you stand up?"

Paul got up and took a few steps, leaning on his contact for support. He straightened his jacket and felt for his wallet.

"Well, it wasn't a robbery. I still have my money and ID cards." Then he noticed something missing.

"Oh no. The letter is gone."

"Describe the man to me while we ride back to your hotel. My car isn't far from here. Can you walk?"

"I think so."

"Any broken bones?"

"I don't think so. How will I face Gabriella's father without her note?"

"Just tell her what I read to you and don't worry about it. My car is across the street."

While Mango pushed the key into the driver's-side door, Paul leaned carefully against the car. Sliding into the front seat, he put his head back while his savior started the engine.

"I'll try to get some information for you for tomorrow. Meet me on the beach as planned. I think I know where I might look for your letter."

"How can I thank you enough, Tonio? I never imagined getting in this deep, just to deliver a note for a woman I just met."

"Forget it. Just part of my job, but be more careful in the future. And from now on, call me Mango. Use only my code name for any contact with me, written or verbal."

They parted at Paul's hotel and he gingerly climbed the stairs, holding on to the slender railing. The telephone was ringing as he opened the door. He shuffled over to pick up the receiver. A deep voice spoke quickly.

"Leave the Rojas woman alone and get out of Cuba."

"Who is this?" he yelled, but the caller hung up.

Switching on the light, he noticed that his luggage has been moved. Had the room been searched while he was out, or had it been the housekeeper? Nothing seemed to be missing. Seeing the fax transmission, he scooped it up, noticing the time stamp at the top: 10:16 p.m. The short note read:

Roberto Santiago, the girl's brother, killed in Bogotá March 13, 1990. Local sources point to a drug connection…. Santiago ranch bought by Carlos Rojas in April 1990…used as rebel headquarters. Rojas seen in Havana today. Father flew to Colombia at 3 p.m.; son took private jet to Puerto Rico. Be careful. Research

Throwing it down on the bed, Paul went into the bathroom to wash his face. Then he found the aspirin bottle in his luggage and took two tablets. Getting into bed, he agonized over whether to tell José that he had lost his niece's note, but decided against it. He would just tell Gabriella's father what Mango had told him, with the hope that he understood. Paul began to try to analyze the situation and realized that he was in deeper than he wanted to be, simply because he felt something for this woman. Having people tell him to be careful just made him more fearful. He fell asleep trying to devise a plan to free himself from the crazy Cuban labyrinth.

****

Paul woke up to bright sunshine streaming in through the patio window, and he took a quick shower. Remembering to wear his swim trunks, he pulled on a pair of shorts and a light shirt and went downstairs. It was already oppressively warm as he stepped through the revolving door and walked down the street, trying to remember where the National Theatre was located. Passing a small shop that sold drinks, he bought some sweet Cuban coffee and sipped it as he hummed a song he had heard on the radio to calm himself. Then, he passed a small inner courtyard behind a grand stone house, its façade crumbling and decaying from lack of care. A large group of elderly Cubans milled about, trying out new dance steps and chatting with one another. Several couples in the center glided past the iron gates while executing a flawless rhumba, their faces full and shining with contentment.

"Excuse me, do you speak English?"

The man nodded his head and slowly came closer to the gate.

"Can you tell me the way to the National Theater?"

Lowering his voice, he looked left and right before saying in perfect English

"The theater is closed on Sunday, sir. It is four blocks down past the consulate building."

"Thank you."

Paul continued down the street until he found the impressive government building, and waited patiently near the front door of the theater. Soon he saw José drive to the curb in a beat-up little Lada, those Russian pieces of tin they call cars. He hopped in and tried to appear normal, while worrying about the one item he'd lost and should have been carrying.

"How are you this fine morning, José?"

"Can you drive this machine, Mr. Brennan? I am better behind a rudder than a steering wheel!"

"Sure. Stop the car and I can slide over." José screeched to a jerky halt and jumped out. Paul took the wheel, glad to have some activity to keep his mind occupied.

"You'll have to direct me, José."

As Paul drove, he mentioned seeing the elderly ballroom dancers. "You don't see that so much in the States."

"Older Cubans take dancing very seriously. It is in their blood and is one of the social activities that the government condones."

"That show last night was really something else. How do those girls walk around with all of that bling on their heads?"

"Bling? What is that?"

"You know, showy flashy costumes."

"Oh...I don't approve of that sort of thing. That garbage is just for the tourists. It is nothing but a way to get some money from them. No, I don't like to see those shows."

As Paul listened to his comments, he wondered how José's conservative attitude had affected Gabriella as a teenager when she lived under his roof. It must have been hard for her, he thought. José did have a keen eye for detail and began to explain the intricacies of sailing. He painted a description of Lima that Paul could almost taste and smell.

As they neared the beach, Paul became anxious to take a swim.

"I am wearing trunks. Where can we take a dip?"

José pointed to a clearing and they parked the car there. Paul could hear the waves and see the blue water as they walked across the road and then under some trees. The dirt became fine sand and Paul unzipped his trousers. Peeling off his shirt and making a pile under a palm, he and José walked to the edge and felt the warm, salty water cover their feet.

José splashed in and dove under a wave. Paul followed him. The water felt wonderful and soothing, and he swam out a bit more and turned around to get a good look at the beach. Searching for a tree that might be shading Mango, he held up a hand to shade his eyes from the sun. There to the left, secluded and private, he saw someone standing in a red bathing suit next to a large bush. A good place to change, he thought, as he began to swim in. He passed José.

"I am going in," he yelled and José nodded.

Grabbing his clothes and feeling the hot burning sand on his feet, he sprinted over to the protection of the shade and moved behind the bush to remove his trunks. He saw Mango sitting on the sand a bit farther off, reading a newspaper. He walked over to him after dressing.

"I have something for you Brennan," the voice announced from behind the paper.

A hand emerged with Gaby's note.

"Where did you get it?"

"Never mind. You owe me one. Just be careful."

"When I got back to my room last night I got a phone call. Someone warned me to get out of Cuba."

"Whoever that was won't give up until you leave. Meet me for dinner at the Morocco tonight. I may have more information. Better get back to your man. He's coming out of the water."

"You're a lifesaver, Mango. See you around seven."

José decided to drive and hopped into the driver's seat. They sped along a highway for a bit and then turned off down a dusty, overgrown lane, and made a few twists until they found a wide, gravel driveway. Stopping at the gate they suddenly heard shouts. Several armed men came out of the bushes and they were greeted in a jumble of Spanish and English. The gate was opened and they drove through slowly, parking in front of an old villa. José and Paul slowly advanced to the front door.

A plump, tired-looking woman opened the front door. She kissed José on both cheeks and ushered them quickly into the house without saying a word to them. Paul looked around. Everything seemed to belong to another era. He suddenly felt like he was thirteen again when he noticed the old, light oak TV/stereo console, and a worn, foam-green sectional sofa next to a step table filled with dated magazines and a pink kidney-shaped ashtray. He followed them as they hurried through corridors that led toward the back of the house, and made a left turn to go through the kitchen. The air was laced with the aroma of bay leaf mingled with basil. Someone was cooking a wonderful meal. The woman opened a door off the kitchen and they all went out to a patio overlooking the ocean. Paul looked out across the water and then sat down at a glass-topped table, while José walked down to the cabana and went in. Paul closed his eyes and wondered how to approach Gabriella's father.

"I am Maria," the plump woman suddenly announced. She touched his arm and offered him a margarita. Paul took it and nodded his head in thanks. Then he heard voices. Turning around, he saw the two brothers and immediately noticed the resemblance. Gabriella's father was shorter and thinner than José, and the lines in his rugged face were clearly the result of worry and discontent, not of sun-drenched hours on a boat like his brother's. As he came closer, Paul stood up and saw warm brown eyes hopeful for good news. Ricardo's smile was tinged with sadness just like Gaby's. He extended a calloused, tanned hand for Paul to shake, and then, as if overwhelmed with joy, embraced him.

"Señor Brennan, I am so pleased to meet you. Thank you for coming. You must excuse my English. It is not so good like my brother's. He will translate for me."

"I think your English is quite understandable, sir" replied Paul as he took his seat again next to José and opposite Ricardo.

"I learn many year ago but forget. I am farmer, not city man like my brother José."

"I am only sorry I cannot speak Spanish better. You know how Americans hate to learn languages! I will speak slowly so José can translate for me."

At that, his face darkened and his eyes became even sadder.

"Señor Brennan, tell me about my only daughter. Is she all right?"

"Yes she is. I met her several days ago in St. Thomas. She is fine and sends her love to you. She was very insistent that I take this note to you, because she is worried about your health." Paul smiled and patted Ricardo's arm.

As José translated, Paul pulled the envelope from his pocket and pushed it across the table to him. His eyes brightened when he saw her handwriting, and with shaky hands he carefully opened the envelope and removed the note. He stared at it for a few moments and then began to read. Paul got up and walked away to give him privacy. As he watched the waves rolling in to the shoreline, he thought he heard Ricardo weeping. Turning around, he saw José put his arm around his brother to comfort him. There were so many questions Paul wanted to ask this man, and so many things he wanted to tell him.

"My brother is overcome with happiness at hearing from his daughter, and sad to be reminded of the loss of his son," José explained, and beckoned for Paul to return to the table.

"Señor Santiago, I am very sorry about the death of your son. I'm sure that Gabriella shares your sorrow." Paul was trying to find a way to allow her father to tell him more.

"Sometimes it helps to speak about these things."

Ricardo cleared his throat and raised watery eyes to look at Paul. José struggled to translate fast enough.

"Señor Brennan, I am most grateful for this message. I know it was not easy for you to come here. Cuba can be a forbidding place for an American. My daughter and I have not spoken since we left home. She thinks I blame her for my son's death. I do not. I only blame myself for letting her become involved with the Rojas family. It is their fault that he is dead."

"Mr. Santiago, did Carlos kill your son?"

Pausing a bit, he cleared his throat and began to speak.

"I am convinced that Carlos killed him, whether or not his own hand did the job. He probably had someone else plant the bomb."

"Why would Gabriella's husband want to kill him?"

49

"The answer to that is very involved. You must understand the situation in Colombia, and in many places in Central and South America. Drug money rules lives, and if people get in the way, they are simply removed."

"But I still don't understand. Was Roberto working against Carlos's operation?"

"Roberto and I felt the same way about drugs. They are powerful substances which control and destroy. We did not think that the wealth earned from the sales was worth all the human destruction and havoc. Before Gabriella's mother died, I was peacefully cultivating my coffee crop and was not interested in growing coca. Carlos changed all that."

Paul drew a deep breath and asked him to continue.

"My daughter was very sad when she returned from Lima. Her mother was gone and she was lost. She had no direction. Then she met Carlos, and she suddenly became content. A daughter's happiness is the most important thing for a father, Mr. Brennan. I thought I was buying her a stable future when I made the arrangement with Rojas for her education. Instead of having an honorable profession, she only learned about greed and corruption. Now she is caught in Carlos's web. I have given my poor Gabriella only heartache. I am just relieved that her mother was spared this grief."

Seeing that her father was wracked by guilt over his decision to "give" Gabriella to Rojas, Paul wanted to tell him that she still cared.

"Forgive me, sir, but I know that your daughter loves you as much as she did before your son died. She speaks of you endearingly and was so concerned about you. She begged me to come to you."

"I pray that you are right. Her note says that she blames herself for her brother's death, and I must see her and put her mind at rest. She should not accept the blame for her husband's deed."

"Do you have proof that it was one of Carlos's men who put the bomb in Roberto's car?"

"If you know Carlos and his father, you don't need proof. My son was fighting for me to keep my land and to farm it the way I wished. It took my son's death to make me realize that Carlos's price was too high and that he would not stop until he succeeded. I had to sell my land to pay off debts from my wife's illness and save what was left of my family. Now Carlos owns the property and uses it for his filthy business."

Paul could see sadness slowly being replaced by hate for the Rojas family and all that it stood for. Ricardo's eyes darkened and his fists began to clench.

"When I think of how he destroyed my family! He took Gabriella away from me, killed my Roberto, and turned Manuel into a savage. Little Tomás is the only one who has been spared."

"Who is Manuel?"

José spoke up, seeing that his brother was too overcome to continue.

"Manuel is Gabriella's brother. He was always sensitive and was most affected by his mother's death. Carlos wanted to take him into the business, but when Roberto was killed, Manuel became depressed and ran away. He lives in Bogotá in the sewers."

"In the sewers?"

Gabriella's father got up and looked into Paul's eyes.

"My son is a *gamino*. He eats garbage and lives with the rats under the streets. When he needs money, he sells dollars for *intis* on the street. Filthy drug dollars that Carlos helps put into circulation. My Manuel doesn't want any help. He just feels that life underground is preferable to the stinking world in the streets above his safe little haven. It breaks my heart. Now he fights against the opposition to drugs by learning to set bombs. He hates the police and informs on them because the authorities could care less about these poor children who have no future."

José began to speak in English.

"Ricardo has asked Carlos to intercede, but he has told us that the boy wants no help from him. Manuel is supposedly addicted to

51

cocaine, which he can get easily. So you see how all of my brother's family has been tainted by the Rojas hand, and how sad it all is."

"Have you ever considered working with the American government? They are trying to convict people like Carlos. I'm sure they would be willing to try and help you if I asked them."

"I have no faith in any government, especially the US. Their efforts are useless. They waste their money here. No, I don't see how they can help my poor Gabriella."

"Please think about it. I can talk to a colleague here in Cuba. He might be able to help Manuel at least."

"If they could help save Manuel, I would be grateful. But I doubt that anything can be done to Carlos. He is too powerful."

"I will speak to my friend tonight when I meet him for dinner."

Suddenly the door to the patio opened, and Maria walked in.

"Lunch is ready," she announced while she began to clear the drink glasses and set the table.

"Please honor us with staying for lunch, Señor Brennan. Our cook makes an excellent fish stew. She will be hurt if you do not try it. José will get you back in time for your dinner appointment."

"I'd like that." Paul thought it might be a good opportunity to learn more about this family into which he was being drawn. As he reached for a slice of bread and held out his wine glass for some sangria, he wondered what Mango would say about all of this.

CHAPTER 7

The lobby of Hotel Morocco was buzzing with activity as Paul strode through the front entrance. Tourists out for some Friday night fun surrounded the bar area, which looked like a scene from the movie *Casablanca*. Whirling ceiling fans and high-backed rattan chairs lent an exotic flavor to the aging walls and faded Turkish carpets. Overweight Russian wives in tight summer dresses held mixed vodka drinks in their pudgy hands, while conversing animatedly with their husbands and girlfriends. Cuban waiters on a break congregated in a small corner, where bits of Spanish could be heard between sounds of guitar strings and softly sung ballads.

Paul quickly sprinted up the back stairs to Mango's room and knocked on the door. Hearing some shuffling inside, he waited until the door opened a crack and then was flung wide open.

"You're a bit early, Brennan. Come in while I finish this report. Have a drink." He motioned to the sitting room and Paul poured himself a Scotch from the generous liquor cabinet built into the wall. He peered into the bedroom, its cathedral ceilings reflecting light from the massive windows that opened onto a small balcony facing the Malecón. Mango sat in front of a computer typing furiously. Suddenly he grabbed the phone and slowly repeated "command center," which immediately connected him to headquarters. He was surrounded by the latest technology. The quiet little fax machine began to transmit a message into Mango's computer instead of loudly announcing its presence with rustling paper like Paul's did.

"I wish I had a fax as small and quiet as yours, Mango."

"It scans as well as copies to my screen. It's the latest on the market."

"Our government never gave me such fancy equipment. My fax makes so much noise I thought someone was burglarizing my hotel room one night."

"Why did they put you in that dump of a hotel by the way?"

"They explained that it would be more secure and unobtrusive to have me stay in a small hotel frequented by visitors from communist countries. You certainly have a nice setup here, Mango."

"I assure you they get their money's worth out of me. Let's go downstairs and have dinner. I've got a lot to discuss with you. If you're interested, you could also have a setup like mine."

They walked down to the ornate dining room and ordered some appetizers.

"Any more calls telling you to scram?" Mango opened his menu and began to read while he waited for the answer.

"No. No calls. But I've been out most of the day. I finally met the girl's father. He's a sincere, honest man who has a strong belief in God and in justice."

"See any of Carlos's men there?"

"I don't think so. Well, there were guards when we drove up. I don't speak much Spanish so I can't tell you much."

The appetizers arrived and Mango picked out a few.

"That's too bad. But you'll still be all right for this job we have in mind for you."

"What job? I'm ready to go to Puerto Rico to see Gabriella."

"Oh, you'll be going to Puerto Rico, but if you are willing to help our government, you may be doing more travelling."

Paul bit into a fried, breaded fish tidbit on a toothpick.

"Just what does Brian Matthews have in mind, Mango?"

"Our government has a little proposition for you. They need to get some information about Carlos, and since you have already built a rapport with three of the family members, you are the most logical, if not the best choice."

"Choice for what?"

"The US would like to put Carlos out of business. They need someone to infiltrate his operation and send back information that they can use to legally charge him. You would be monitoring his activities and following him if necessary to gather facts. Getting friendly with his family is the first step, and you have already done that."

"How heavily do they want me to be involved? I'm primarily a journalist who happens to be on their payroll for occasional minor and nonthreatening investigations. Not something like this!"

"The DEA is very interested in having you on board. They are willing to release you from the newspaper duties and will guarantee your job when this is all over."

"And when will this be *all over*?"

"Who knows? They just wanted me to offer the proposal. Look, they aren't twisting your arm. If you won't agree to do it, they'll just find someone else. Let's order."

Mango snapped his finger in the air and a waiter hurried over. He ordered two fish dinners in Spanish along with some red wine.

"They make the best paella here, Paul. You'll love it. I ordered a good red wine, too."

"Thanks. I hope I can enjoy it now that you've made me uneasy about all this business."

Mango leaned closer toward him and spoke in a lower tone.

"What you don't know, Brennan, is how dangerous Carlos's operation is to our efforts to control the flow of drugs to the US. The president is making this a focus of his campaign and wants some action down here. You'd be doing a great service to our country as well as to South America."

"I'm not so sure I agree with you. I spent all afternoon with the Santiago brothers. Do you know that most people in Peru are starving? They can only look at meat through a shop window and don't have enough money to buy it? Poppy plantations are the only way to survive for some people. They are so incensed about the poverty that they try to undermine any effort for positive change. They bomb establishments and kill people and continue to destroy any hope for the future."

"I see that someone has been filling your head with a lot of nonsense. A lot of damage has been attributed to that rebel group called the Shining Path. But don't believe everything the girl's father and uncle tell you. They may not be reliable sources."

Mango leaned away to allow the waiter to pour the wine, and he picked up his glass and held it up for a toast.

"Here's to our future collaboration, Paul."

Paul took a sip and put his glass down.

"No, Mr. Santiago is very much against drugs. He is even willing to ask our government to help free his son from his life in the sewers."

"I thought his son was killed."

"He has another son who ran away and lives underground in Bogotá. His life is in danger and I offered your assistance."

"That was generous of you! Why did you think I'd be willing to help him?"

"I know you have good connections in the State Department and I just felt I had to try and offer him something. If you could have seen his tears, I know you would have been moved to do something."

"I think you are one of those bleeding-heart liberals, Brennan. Look, I'm not sure what we can do, but if you cooperate on this project to get information on Carlos, I'm sure State will look into the matter."

Paul buttered some garlic bread. "I don't like being bribed, Mango, but I do want to help Gabriella's family."

The waiter placed hot, steaming plates in front of them.

"I have to work in strange and manipulative ways in this business, Brennan. Especially here in Cuba."

"By the way, did you ever find out exactly what Rojas wanted from the military?"

"Our contact assures us that Rojas asked Castro to provide arms for the rebels fighting against the DEA officers. He is also throwing in some free medical treatment in exchange for drug dollars. It's a profitable venture for Cuba, since those are the two things they have to use as bargaining chips. We're pretty sure they closed the deal."

Paul sipped his wine thoughtfully. Then he gave Mango a serious look.

"I wonder just how much Gabriella knows about Carlos's operation."

"That is exactly what we want you to find out. Get to know her intimately and gather as much information about him as possible, in the shortest time possible. A tall order, but not without fringe benefits." Mango laughed.

"You mean you want me to use her and then say 'so long'?"

If that's what it takes, yes," Mango replied as he shoved forkfuls of rice into his mouth.

"I don't know that I can do that. I already feel something for this woman. The better I get to know her, the harder it will be to betray her."

"Perhaps it will be easier to use her once you find out more about the Rojas's activities. Remember, she is also a Rojas. Family ties are strong bonds in Latin countries."

"I'll think hard about it tonight. When do you need an answer?"

"Headquarters wants to know by Monday morning at the latest so they can find a replacement if you don't agree. They'll fax you some details tonight. Let me know as soon as you decide. I'm instructed to keep tabs on you 'from afar' as they say. I'll be in whatever country you find yourself, if not the city. You'll always be able to reach me or one of our other South American contacts. What are the plans to get you to Puerto Rico?"

"They want to take me by boat and they are waiting for favorable weather conditions. They will contact me soon. They are considering a trip on Sunday morning."

The waiter removed their plates and brought the flan and coffee.

"They probably have a boat waiting. You may be asked to leave Havana as early as tomorrow afternoon to be able to put to sea early Sunday morning. Think fast, Brennan. You may only have tonight to mull things over. Go back to your hotel and dream of your Gabriella."

"That's not hard. I seem to think of her a lot already."

"Look, Paul. Take my advice. Don't let any woman control you, especially one like this one. Our work is too important to be compromised. Trust no one but yourself."

"And you of course, Mango?"

Mango pulled out his wallet and threw his American Express card down on the table next to the bill.

"I said *no one*, Brennan. To be absolutely sure, trust only your instincts."

"Thanks for dinner, Mango. I'll be in touch."

"I'll be waiting to hear from you. Remember to use the codes."

With a nod, Paul got up and made his way to the lobby to leave and find a cab.

CHAPTER 8

The little green rusty Lada screeched to a halt promptly at 6 p.m., and Paul jumped in beside José. Gabriella's father sat quietly in the back seat and nodded to him. Paul settled back for the two-hour drive to the coast and tried to look calm.

"So, what kind of boat are we taking?" he asked.

There was a strange, eerie silence from both men, and he decided not to pursue that question.

"How long will the trip take?"

José turned and smiled slyly, revealing his broken crooked teeth "Are you missing my niece, Mr. Brennan?

Paul smiled and laughed.

"I'm just trying to make conversation."

Thinking that these two were strangely silent, he decided to open the English language newspaper he'd brought with him. He started to think how nice it would be to see Gaby, and to talk to Mango on Monday night when he was due to arrive. Mango promised to contact him as soon as his plane landed. Paul had decided to help them get information on Carlos since they offered to help Manuel. He was so engrossed in the newspaper article that he hardly noticed when the car slowed and came to an abrupt halt. He looked up. They were on a landing strip and in front of them stood a private jet. Two men holding machine guns walked toward the car.

"What is this? Paul shouted. "What are we doing at an airport? I thought we were going by boat?"

"Last-minute change in plans" José replied while he lifted the two small suitcases out of the back seat.

The guards began to speak to Ricardo, and José ushered him up the stairs. At the top, a short, well-dressed man appeared, his dark hair slicked back with pomade. As Paul passed him, the sweet smell of heavy cologne stung his nostrils, and his eye caught the man's sparkling gold watch and link bracelet dangling from hairy, pink-cuffed wrists. In a heavily accented voice he greeted him.

"Welcome to the Rojas family jet. I hope you will be comfortable."

The interior was plush red velvet, and Paul sank into a white, fur-covered swivel chair and kicked off his shoes. Hearing the doors clang shut he looked out of the window to see one of the guards drive off in the Lada. He turned back to see José coming toward him with a drink.

"Here is something to calm you, Mr. Brennan." He held out a glass of Scotch and water. "I want you to meet someone." He called the well-dressed man over.

"Allow me to present Eduardo Rojas."

Paul stood up and stretched out his hand as Eduardo offered a handshake.

"I am Gabriella's brother-in-law." They both sat down.

"So you are Carlos's brother" Paul said tentatively.

"Yes. You will meet him when we land. He insisted on sending his private plane to pick up his father-in-law. What is your connection with Gabriella, Mr. Brennan?"

"I met her in St. Thomas. She asked me to deliver a message to her father in Cuba. She wanted to see me afterward, and since I had an assignment in Puerto Rico I thought…"

Eduardo raised his eyebrows. "Assignment?"

"Yes, I am a journalist for a large American newspaper. We're doing a report on the issue of statehood for Puerto Rico and I need to interview some people about it."

Eduardo looked at Paul intently. Paul had the distinct feeling that Eduardo knew all about how he had met Gaby before he boarded the jet and didn't believe his "cover."

"This is some jet you have here, Mr. Rojas!" Paul looked around, gulping his Scotch and trying to remain aloof.

"Well, it is Carlos's jet. Please, call me Eduardo. Since you are a friend of Gabriella's and obviously of her father, we must be informal, yes?"

"Of course. Just call me Paul, or PB for short. That's what my colleagues at the paper call me."

Eduardo laughed at that, and as the plane climbed higher into the sky they managed to relax. Paul had to remind himself that he was on a diplomatic mission to gain information on Carlos, so he steered the conversation toward Eduardo's brother.

"I understand Carlos is quite a jet-setter. Doesn't it bother his wife that he is away so often?"

"No. She understands that his business is the key to the future success of the Rojas name. My sister-in-law doesn't complain."

"What exactly is his business, Eduardo?"

"International trade. He spends most of his time in South America, though. I can't give you details since I'm really not included in those high-level negotiations."

"Doesn't it bother you that Carlos gets all the important assignments?"

"No, not at all. You must understand our Latin customs, PB. Our father is chief of operations...what you call the CEO I think in the US. The eldest son receives the honor and the responsibility to carry on when the patriarch is too old or too ill to manage the business. Carlos needs to be properly trained to someday take over. Anyway, I am happy to serve my father and brother in any way I can."

"So you are a loyal son?" Paul shot back.

"There are many rewards for a Rojas, and I enjoy them all," Eduardo proclaimed, as he leaned back and toasted Paul with his glass. "I'm not interested in the business the way Carlos is, and frankly, I wouldn't be comfortable dealing with all that responsibility."

"I understand Carlos and his father recently visited Cuba."

"Yes, they were talking to officials to arrange some exchange or another. But I wasn't told much about that." Eduardo got up to mix himself another drink. Paul wondered if he really knew more and was just being cautious, or if the family really kept him out of the loop on purpose.

"If you want another drink, help yourself. We should be landing shortly and I'm sure you will be invited to dine with us. We always take dinner after 9 p.m. That is also our custom. Excuse me while I speak to Ricardo. We haven't seen each other for a while."

Paul got up and began to pace. Suddenly he felt the jet turn a bit and begin to descend, in preparation for landing. He quickly took his seat and fastened his seatbelt, then picked up a magazine and flipped through the pages nervously.

"We will land very soon, Mr. Brennan," José whispered over his shoulder. "Cuba is really not far from Puerto Rico you see."

Only geographically, Paul thought sarcastically.

"Are Eduardo and your brother really close, José?"

José's face darkened as he watched the two men talk together. "You should know my brother better than that by now. He cannot be rude, but he certainly feels no special bond for any of Carlos's family. Eduardo, though, is the least harmful, I think."

As Paul took mental notes of all this information, the plane dropped its wheels and hit the runway. The soldiers stood at the door and pushed it open soon after the plane stopped. Paul got up and looked out the window. At the bottom of the stairs, a handsome, elegant-looking man with wavy black hair gazed up at the open door. This had to be Gabriella's husband. Her father carefully made his way down the stairs ahead of José and Paul and embraced Carlos. Paul could see a white limo parked a few yards away from the jet, its rear doors wide open like arms to gather them into its depths. He followed José to the bottom of the stairs, and Eduardo followed behind them, as he yelled something in Spanish to his brother.

Carlos and Paul came face-to-face, and Carlos thrust his hand out, gripping Paul's firmly and staring into his eyes. Paul tried to memorize Carlos's features, and they both studied each other until José broke the silence with formal introductions.

"Let me introduce Señor Paul Brennan, Carlos."

"I have heard about you, Mr. Brennan. Thank you for delivering my wife's message. She was very grateful."

"Your wife is very persuasive, Mr. Rojas. And I didn't mind. It gave me a chance to revisit Cuba where I vacationed as a boy."

"Please, call me Carlos. Now we must continue our conversation in the car since Gabriella is anxiously awaiting the arrival of her father."

"All right. I'd feel more comfortable if you called me PB. That's what they call me at work." They all climbed in, and Paul settled back against the red leather interior. The driver accelerated and drove off the runway and onto the main highway that bordered the ocean. Eduardo and Carlos sat next to each other, and Paul found himself seated across from them, between the two Santiago brothers. He was lost in a sea of Spanish until Eduardo opened the mahogany bar and offered him a Scotch.

"Mr. Brennan is here on assignment, Carlos," he reported.

"Oh, you must tell me about your work, PB. I am always interested in hearing about successful professionals like myself, especially if they are American."

"There's not that much to tell. I finished a stint in Romania and needed a break, so I flew to St. Thomas for some R&R. That's where I met your wife."

"Tell me about that encounter," Carlos said after he sipped his drink.

"She sent me a note at my hotel to meet her on a little island, and she and her little brother treated me to a picnic. I must admit I was reluctant to accept the job, but in the end I agreed. I couldn't say no to her."

"Yes, I have that same problem," Carlos said, and he smiled broadly, winking his eye.

Paul thought at that moment that he sounded sincere and seemed to really care for her. He probably spoiled her in his own private way. Paul suddenly felt as if he was intruding on their sacred married life.

"And what is your assignment here in Puerto Rico?"

"I am supposed to interview some people on the question of statehood."

"Ah, yes, that is being discussed, but I seldom stay in one country long enough to connect to their local concerns."

Thinking that this was a good opportunity to begin asking the questions instead of answering them, Paul asked Carlos where his next stop might be. He looked a bit wary, and cautiously replied.

"Wherever my father happens to send me." Then he and Eduardo began talking in Spanish, shutting Paul out of the conversation. Paul lit a cigarette and looked out of the window. Here was a real challenge, he thought. This guy was smart and cool and wouldn't divulge information easily. Perhaps working through Eduardo was the answer, he thought. Maybe Mango was right. Gaby might be the only avenue to the truth.

CHAPTER 9

As Paul peered out into the deepening dusk, the coastal highway began to wind its way gradually up gentle hills and away from the ocean. The barren stretch of road they were following revealed sad scenes of impoverished hovels, which replaced the magnificent high-rise hotels he had noticed when the trip began. With each turn in the road, the settlements became bleaker. Grim-looking, ragged-clothed children stood in front of dilapidated structures and gazed at the sleek white limo as it passed them. He felt an overwhelming sense of shame, and made a mental note to do something for them someday. It would also provide a good article for the newspaper and might be helpful to them. Leaning back against the headrest, he wondered how long it would take to reach their destination. The car slowed as it negotiated an abrupt hairpin turn, and as they climbed higher, the rain seemed to all but disappear. José rolled down the window and cool fresh air filled the living room on wheels. Paul closed his eyes and began to think about Gaby, trying to conjure up her subtle liquid voice and somewhat suspicious but enticing dark eyes.

The car suddenly stopped and they all got out. They began to follow a narrow gravel path lit by tiny green lights set along the grassy edge. As Paul looked ahead in the dusk, he could just discern the outlines of a huge house. Was that her on the balcony? He wasn't sure. Strange birds circled over their heads and began to screech. As they moved closer to the house, he could detect movement ahead, and suddenly the house lights blinked on and he heard that wonderful melodic voice drifting out in the darkness to welcome them.

All of a sudden, he saw Gabriella bounding off the porch steps, her long hair swinging wildly behind her. She melted into her father's arms and began to speak very softly to him, leading him toward the little gazebo to the left of the house. Carlos proceeded to enter the house without saying anything to his wife, and Eduardo told Paul to follow him. He was led to a small cottage toward the back of the house.

"You can freshen up here, PB. Meet us at the house in a half hour for dinner."

Paul began to unpack and then remembered that he needed to contact Mango. He took his pager and clicked a few buttons, tapping out a coded message that he had arrived by plane. In a minute, the pager beeped and a coded reply flashed on the screen. "Sit tight. Message at midnight."

Paul sent the received code and added a reminder alert to check it at midnight for Mango's message. Then he deactivated the pager. He took a quick shower and changed into fresh clothes. When he carefully parted the curtains covering the small window, they revealed a glimmering, white full moon, which sent streaks of light into the tiny, dim room. Paul turned on a lamp beside the bed and finished unpacking his overnight bag. Sliding it under the bed, he turned to open the door, when he noticed a white, folded note on the floor. Bending down to pick it up, he recognized the handwriting and quickly unfolded it.

Meet me at midnight in my room 2nd floor, second room on left. GR

The midnight hour was popular tonight he thought, as he walked slowly up the hilly path toward the house. The brilliant moon lit his way and he was grateful for the help in unknown terrain. Gaby's note brought back all the wonderful, warm feelings he had experienced when they had met, and he was impatient to be alone with her. He had to admit that seeing her fly into her father's arms had made him a bit jealous that she hadn't fallen into his first.

Carlos had seemed to all but ignore her, so atypical for a loving, affectionate husband who had been away from her, he thought. Then it struck him! How could he meet her with her husband so nearby? His palms began to sweat as he grasped the doorknob and entered the well-lit foyer. The crystal chandelier above his head swung a bit as he closed the front door. As he looked up, he saw a uniformed guard at the top of the stairs, motioning him with his gun to walk ahead. He followed the corridor past huge colorful paintings. Turning left toward the sound of Spanish, he entered a spacious dining room. Blazing light from the candelabra on the table was reflected in the mirrored walls, and here and there dark blue drapes hid the night.

"Come and join us PB!" shouted Carlos, who was at the head of the table smoking a Cuban cigar while trying to open a bottle of red wine. "I think you know everyone except my bodyguard Julio and our wonderful cook Anna." He pointed out these two with his cigar.

Paul took a seat beside Eduardo and introduced himself.

"Wait until you taste the delicious meal Anna has prepared for us," Carlos boasted while pouring Paul a glass of wine.

"Where is your wife and her father?" Paul asked, noticing their absence.

"He was feeling tired and she is putting him to bed."

"He isn't ill, is he?"

"No, but I'm afraid this was a rather emotional day for him. I am sure that my wife's soothing care will be all he needs."

Paul sipped his wine and noticed that Julio was seemingly studying every face at the table, but in reality was concentrating on his, which was reflected in the mirror in front of the guests.

"I understand you and your father were in Cuba the day I arrived."

"Yes," Carlos said slowly. "We had some business to transact with their government."

"Did you find the Cuban government difficult to deal with?" Paul probed, hoping to open a dialog with him.

Eduardo began to laugh. "Remember the time Castro wanted to exchange some prisoners...?"

Carlos shot him a menacing glance and cut him off.

"Mr. Brennan doesn't want to hear those stories. You must forgive my little brother, Paul. He is never serious. Fidel is a courageous fighter and has done much for Cuba. My father and I have never found him difficult. Our little business ventures are mutually beneficial."

"And what does Cuba have that Colombia wants?" Paul asked.

"Cheap vodka and rhumba bands!" answered Gabriella's sweet voice as she entered the room. The ruffles of her red, low-cut blouse revealed just a bit of the crease between her large breasts, and her long black skirt almost covered her boots and brushed the ground as she glided over to the table. Seeing Paul, she gasped his name with delight and sat down across from him.

"Paolo, I must thank you deeply for doing what I asked. You have brought my father to me!"

"Well, I think your husband had more to do with that than I did."

"Yes, but you had the courage to take my letter to him. I will always be grateful to you." Warmth radiated from her eyes as they spoke to his, and they embraced in a long, intense glance.

"How is your father?" he asked in a lower tone.

"He is sleeping now. He needs to rest." Turning to Carlos, she murmured

"We had a long talk. He told me he never blamed me for my brother's death."

"Your brother was an unfortunate casualty of war, my dear." Carlos replied in a loud, brash voice, as Anna spooned some gazpacho into Carlos's white porcelain bowl. Pointing his large soup spoon at Gabriella, he pompously proclaimed "If he had listened to me, he would be sitting here with us tonight, enjoying a fine dinner."

"You will never understand how my brother felt about the situation in our country or how my father feels about losing his land." Gabriella answered icily.

"Your father would still be in Peru on his ranch if he had done what I wanted. He is an old, stubborn fool who cannot understand the modern world. Coffee is not profitable anymore. People must learn to adjust to the times," Carlos insisted while stabbing his fork into a piece of the paella on the tray Anna held out to him. "Don't you agree, Paolo?" Carlos asked sarcastically as he swirled the red wine in his glass.

"I think that people can only be productive if they believe in what they are doing. Apparently Gabriella's father wasn't convinced that it was right for him to follow your ideas, whatever they were. I think that is what your wife is trying to say."

"Carlos does not understand because he has never lost anything or anyone he cared about" Gabriella commented bitterly.

José broke the silence. "Roberto did what he thought was right. He can be at peace knowing he did not betray his beliefs. But Carlos has a point. Peruvians are starving. If coca farming was replaced, many peasants would be without any income. Forgive me, Mr. Brennan, but I do not think your country understands. The US would do better to deal with the drug problem in their own country, not in ours."

Paul looked at Gaby. The corners of her mouth turned into a gentle smile and her eyes twinkled.

"I think we should think of more pleasant things!" she suddenly blurted out. "Tomorrow afternoon we should all have a picnic on the beach."

"That sounds great to me." Paul replied. "I'd like to see this area in the daylight."

"Gabriella can show you the area, PB. Perhaps you can both take her father out for some fresh air."

Gabriella looked longingly at Paul. "Why do you call him PB, Carlos?" she asked, not taking her eyes away from Paul.

"Your husband wanted me to be informal, so I told him that colleagues at the paper call me by my initials for short."

"Oh, I see," she murmured. "What does 'for short' mean?" she asked coyly.

Before Paul could answer, Anna whispered something in Carlos's ear and he abruptly stood up and motioned for Julio to follow him.

"You must excuse me. I have an urgent telephone call." He stalked out of the room with his bodyguard on his heels.

Gabriella looked relieved, and held her wine glass up near the candle flame, tipping the glass so that the red liquid swirled from side to side.

"You will like the beach here, Paolo. I will show you the cove where I swim."

"After dinner I would like to show Mr. Brennan the rest of the house," declared José. "Did you know that a sea captain once owned this beautiful mansion?"

"No I didn't. I would enjoy seeing the rest of the house." Paul said as he gazed fixedly into Gaby's dancing black eyes, now riveted on his.

"What are your plans for tomorrow, Mr. Brennan? Don't you have to do some work for your paper?"

"Yes, I need to go into San Juan soon to interview some people. I am waiting for word on that."

Carlos swiftly entered the room and spoke to his wife in Spanish. She quickly got up and left.

"I must return to Bogotá at once. My father has been kidnapped."

José began to speak to him in Spanish and then Carlos told Julio to get the car.

"I apologize for any inconvenience, Paul, but I'm sure you understand my haste. Finish your dinner. I am sure Anna has something wonderful for dessert. Now I must talk to Gabriella. I will see that she is a fine hostess to you tomorrow." With that, he and Eduardo disappeared.

"Does he know who is holding his father?"

"This happens frequently in South America now," José explained. "Just last month I heard that a powerful and wealthy politician was held for ransom. Sometimes they just want money; sometimes they want favors."

"One of my good friends at the newspaper recently completed a six-month investigative report on high-profile kidnapping. I wouldn't want to have to deal with them."

"Gangs of criminals kidnap businessmen because they think they can influence officials. Carlos's father is a very wealthy and important man and has connections with the government. Carlos has been worrying about something like this for a while. Ah, here comes Anna with her famous flan! Eat your dessert and then I will show you the house."

"José, do you really feel that growing coca is essential for Peruvian economic stability? Do you think that the US is doing it all wrong, or did you say that for Carlos's benefit?"

"No, I say it because I know in my heart it is true." He tapped his chest near his heart. "Coca is our nation's largest export. I am afraid if there is no coca harvest there would be a great peasant uprising."

"But what about cocaine? How do you feel when you see so many lives destroyed by drugs?"

"Sometimes it is the only way to escape the horrors of life. Of course I don't like it. But I am also practical, and I see my countrymen dying and starving while trying to work at legitimate farms."

Saying no more, Paul finished his espresso in silence. José put his half-eaten dessert aside and pushed his chair back. Paul rose and followed José out of the dining room to see the mansion. Gabriella had disappeared. They walked along the corridor he had followed earlier and came to a huge sitting room with more paintings and a fireplace. The window looked out onto the back of the house toward the ocean, and Paul could hear the roar of the waves. Then José led him upstairs to a tiny room where a telescope was aimed toward the corner window.

"On clear days you can see El Morro castle from here," José announced. Paul looked out and saw the little cottage below the rise where he was staying. They walked out and down the hall, past what was certainly Gabriella's room. He could smell her perfume, but there was no visible sign of her. Paul felt a bit easier about the planned midnight visit since Carlos would not be around.

"We must be quiet at the other end. Ricardo is sleeping," José warned in a low voice.

They tiptoed past the room and took the back stairs. Paul looked at his watch.

"Thanks for the tour, José, but I must be getting to bed now."

"Goodnight then. Sleep well. I will see you tomorrow at breakfast."

Hurrying down to the cottage, he glanced at his watch again. It was 11:15. He needed to contact Mango right away. As soon as he was safely inside, he pulled the curtains closed and tapped a few code numbers into the pager. He waited. No response. Where was Mango? Kicking off his shoes, he stretched across the bed and grabbed a week-old newspaper covering the bottom of a magazine basket near the night table. Seeing that it was in Spanish he tossed it aside and began to finish unpacking. Suddenly his pager beeped. A code appeared on the little screen as he waited for the message. "Meet me San Juan airport 5 p.m. tomorrow. Executive lounge. Read?"

Paul quickly keyed in the secret code which meant understood. Then he sent another.

"Jorge Rojas kidnapped tonight. Carlos to Bogotá. Should I follow?"

A few seconds later, digital numbers flashed and he saw "orders in SJ."

Nothing to do now but wait. Suddenly noticing the stale, humid air, he pulled the curtains back to reveal the full moon, and he forced the tiny window open. A slight breeze wafted over him and the smell of the sea reminded him of the beach date he had with Gaby tomorrow. Excitement began to overwhelm him. He had felt empty for so long and needed to be with someone special. He looked at himself in the mirror over the sink in the bathroom. A few grey hairs mingled with the sandy brown, and a wrinkle had imprinted its crease at the edge of one of his tired eyes.

Too much travelling. Too much fast food. Too many airplanes. Too many late-night deadlines requiring rewrites in front of a computer screen. When would he be satisfied with his little walk-up in New York City? Why did the thrill of seeing new places seem less enticing now? He splashed on some cologne and turned away from the mirror as if to escape himself for a few hours. Tonight he would try to seduce someone's wife! He had to admit he was a bit frightened at the prospect of getting caught, yet that was exactly what made the escapade so inviting. He tried to remember that he was on a mission for his country. Information hunting…. Espionage! What a crazy game. All he really wanted was to have Gaby next to him for awhile.

Locking the door behind him, he started to climb toward the house. How would he get in the front door? What about the guard? These questions only heightened his passion. He turned the knob slowly. The door was unlocked. No guard was in sight as he stole rapidly up the stairs and down the hall to her room. He knocked twice and waited impatiently, hoping that there was no guard at the other end of the hallway, or if there was, that he didn't hear him. The door slowly opened and Gaby took his arm. He stepped inside and without saying a word, she quickly checked the hall before pushing the door closed.

"Is there anyone watching us?" Paul whispered. She put her finger to his lips to silence him and pressed her ear to the door. Then she smiled and walked to the other side of the room near the window.

"The moon will protect us Paolo," and she calmly closed the drapes. "Would you like some wine or cognac?"

"Cognac," he uttered softly, as he looked around the room. It was simple but elegant, like the woman handing him the drink.

"How did you manage to keep the front door unlocked? Where is the guard?"

"Anna is a friend as well as a servant. She can be trusted. I told her to leave the door unlocked. The guard always takes a short break at midnight, and since Julio and Eduardo are with my husband, there is no one else to watch the house."

"No other guards to protect Carlos?"

"You seem to think he is more powerful and important than he really is, Paolo. He is only a South American businessman."

"Oh. I thought he moved mountains and controlled lives."

"No, he only thinks he does." She sipped her cognac and moved over to sit on the edge of the bed.

"What did he mean tonight about your father being stubborn?"

"Carlos wanted to turn my father's coffee plantation into a coca ranch. He is building a processing plant on the site of my mother's grave. That is hurting my father terribly. My father's land has been in our family for six generations, and he always wanted his oldest son to continue the business when he got too old. He used to say that he would one day sit on the veranda and watch his grandchildren play near the slopes where he worked as a boy. He wanted it to remain as it was...a coffee plantation. But Carlos did not agree. He first tried to bargain with my father. Then he tried to use me to get to him. When I refused, he offered my brother a job. My father only gave in after Roberto was killed, and he knew Carlos would get his way in the end. Father became bitter and sad, blaming himself for my brother's death. Manuel ran away from him and he was alone. The bill collectors were demanding their money, and Father just lost the will to fight for the land."

"What does Carlos really do, Gaby?"

"I don't know details, but I know enough. He supports the production of cocaine any way he can, and helps to transport it to the US. He fights against the anti-drug forces and is buying guns and ammunition from Cuba to arm the rebels. Castro is throwing in some medicine to sweeten the deal."

"Cuba is aiding the drug lords here in Colombia?"

"They have been helping Carlos's father for a long time. Jorge Rojas has many old friends there."

Paul looked into Gaby's eyes. "Did Carlos kill Roberto?" he asked quietly.

Tears began to fall from her cheeks, and he was almost sorry he had asked.

"I don't know for sure. But I feel more distant from my husband every day when I think of how he treats my family."

Putting his arm around her shoulders, Paul gently placed his hand on her cheek and turned her sad face toward his.

"Don't cry my darling," he whispered as he pulled her closer and their lips met. Her almost silent sobs were slowly replaced by a tender outpouring of desire, and he could feel her body react to his advances. They stretched out and he loosened his collar and unbuttoned and removed his shirt. The moon shot its radiant beams across her face as he began to undress her. She reached up for him and he held her long hair between his fingers, twisting it with his hand to bring her face closer to his. Her tongue playfully searched his ear and he buried his head between her large, full breasts. Her hot breath grew more insistent. Suddenly she stopped and became very still. "What is it?" he asked.

"Shhhh," she whispered. Then he heard heavy footsteps at the other end of the hall. The guard walked slowly past her room, stopped outside for a moment, and then continued down the stairs.

"He's gone for a while," she said.

"How and when will I leave you in the morning?"

"It will be safe if you go before the sun rises. Come back for breakfast at eight." She rolled on top of him and spread her thighs, deftly lowering herself on top of him. He pressed her body tightly against his and was soon in his own fantasy, swimming with her in a magic pool on French cap. She moaned softly and he slowly turned her over on her back, pushing himself further inside. Her hands stroked his hair and she opened her mouth wide to allow his tongue entrance. Pulling him closer, she spoke his name softly in measured gasps. Her soft pubic hair brushed his thighs as he began to move back and forth more vigorously, and he moved his mouth to her breasts to surround her hard nipples with his lips. The moon's glow mixed with theirs and they were finally one for just a moment in time. He gently pulled away from her and took her in his arms, showering her neck with tiny kisses, smelling her sweet perfume. It felt so good to lie next to her. She sighed and turned over and they both fell into a blissful drowsy state for a few moments. After a while, she opened her eyes and began to play with his hair.

"Do you know that you have the loveliest cobalt-blue eyes, my darling?"

He leaned up and kissed her.

"Your passion is tinged with tenderness, Paolo. That is good."

"And with Carlos?"

"He was never like this. He is a fierce competitor, even in bed."

"Does Carlos have lovers?"

"Yes, I am sure of it. But he is allowed to, you see. I have accepted it, as all Latin women must. He is still my husband, no matter how many whores he takes to bed."

Paul cuddled with her until she fell asleep. Then he drifted off. It was almost five a.m. when a noise woke him, and he dressed quickly. As he kissed her, she whispered the familiar vaya con Dios and turned over to resume her dream. He silently peeked out the door. The guard was dozing, facing away from him, halfway down the stairway that he had used on his way in. Paul slowly crept down the hall to the opposite end and took the back stairs. As he passed the kitchen, Anna saw him but said nothing, her eyes smiling a bit in deference to her mistress, as if she was glad to have helped erase Gabriella's pain for just one night. He found a side door and quickly opened it. The morning salt air filled his lungs, and he raced down the hill and over to the little cottage. His mission successfully completed, he fell into a deep sleep after setting his alarm for 7:30 a.m.

CHAPTER 10

Daylight was finally beginning to break into the dusty, filthy basement of the warehouse on the outskirts of Bogotá. Jorge Rojas stirred, twisting uncomfortably in his awkward position, trying to free himself from the ropes that cut into the tanned, wrinkled skin of his wrists. Heavy footsteps told him his captors were arriving.

"Good morning, Señor Rojas. We brought you a little breakfast." The guard let out a derisive laugh as he shoved a dead mouse on a dirty broken plate under the nose of Carlos's father.

"I beg you to let me speak with my son. He will arrange everything. You will get what you want."

"Shut up you bastard. Your son will soon find out about this, and I'm sure he will want to free his important father. But he will do it on our terms, not yours. See how you like taking orders!" He pushed the mouse into Jorge Rojas's face and kicked him several times, causing the old man to grimace in pain and yell out for him to stop.

▪▪

Carlos replaced the receiver and dejectedly dialed another number, hoping to get some assistance from a friendly government official.

"Hello. Is this Diego Cordera? This is Carlos Rojas, Jorge's son. Have you heard what happened to him? Oh you have...yes, I see. No, I am trying to understand why my father's friends have abandoned him. Just a simple word to the president in favor of "...click. The line went dead. Carlos got up and walked over to the bar to pour himself a Scotch.

"Bastards. They are all no-good selfish dogs. Yesterday they licked my father's boots so they could be elected to office. Today, they want nothing to do with kidnappers. They are all cowards." He knocked back the drink, then walked over to his desk, which sat in a corner of the dimly lit room. He suddenly thought of someone else who might be willing to help. Turning the desk lamp on, he flipped through his address book. Then he dialed the editor of the local newspaper. They had been friends many years ago at school. No one understood the world like Ramón. He could use protection from the Rojas family, and Carlos thought this was the perfect time to offer it.

"Ramón, it is me, Carlos. How are you?"

"Not bad. What have you been up to?"

"I have a great story for you if you are willing to negotiate for it."

"What story? You mean about your father? Our presses are already printing the news for the afternoon edition."

"Don't you think you need protection now that so many newspaper people have been targeted for kidnapping? I could provide you with guards."

"What do you want, Carlos? I don't have time for games."

"The kidnappers want assurance that my father will influence convention delegates to vote to end extradition of drug smugglers to the US. They want me to drop 50 million off somewhere. They plan to hold him until he makes some calls."

"Have they allowed you to speak with him yet?"

"No, but I'm trying to get them to let another family member see him."

"Listen, Carlos. These guys are serious. Give them the money to buy time. It might help if an outsider bargains with them rather than you or Eduardo."

"Would a journalist be a good candidate?"

"Wait a minute. I wasn't suggesting that I get involved."

"Relax. I didn't mean you. But you've given me an idea. Thanks, Ramón."

"Good luck. Let me know what happens. I need all the sensationalist news I can find. Keep in touch."

■■■

Paul waved from the ocean to José and Ricardo, who were sitting on the beach, and pointed in the direction he and Gaby planned to swim. Her tanned, shapely legs cut through the clear, turquoise waves like a knife, leading him to her private cove as he swam behind her. They cavorted in the ocean like two dolphins, swimming next to each other for a while, then following each other, then making a circle. They hugged each other and laughed as the surf broke into their embrace, showering them with foamy spray. Gaby suddenly dove under the water and then jumped up, twisting and turning like a child, her drenched, dark hair falling behind her face and down her back. Paul caught her at the waist and kissed her, and she slowly led him toward the cove's shore. It was deserted and out of sight from anyone's view. They stretched out on white sand under a huge palm, and looked at each other longingly. Then she sat up and tried to wring the water out of her hair.

"Is this not the most beautiful place?" she murmured and Paul had to agree.

"Do you come here often?"

"No, but when I really need to get away from things, it is the best place for me to hide and be alone to think."

"What things are you trying to escape from?"

"Not things, but people; Carlos, his father, his guards. They are always watching me. I needed to hear the sounds of nature and of my own heart, and not to listen to talk about proposals or deadlines."

"Gabriella, I would like to ask you a question."

"Of course, dear Paolo. Anything." Paul looked deeply into her inquisitive eyes.

"Why did you lie to me about your father being with Carlos in Cuba? You knew your husband was in Colombia then."

Her eyes became clouded and sad. "I was afraid you wouldn't deliver my letter if you knew my husband and father were not getting along, so I told you that they were working together. If I had said they weren't speaking to each other, would you have made the trip?"

"I don't know. You were pretty persuasive, though. Have you ever lied to me about anything else? Your father wasn't really exiled, was he? And why couldn't your uncle have delivered the letter?"

"I couldn't trust my uncle. He is too close to Carlos. He seems to think Carlos can do no wrong. Sometimes it is better to trust someone outside of the family, Paolo."

"You might have a point there."

Gaby's eyes suddenly turned fierce and angry and she jumped up, planting her legs firmly on the sand as she had done the day he met her on French cap.

"Please don't treat me like my husband does. Carlos questions me every time he returns from a trip. I had hoped you would be different, Paolo. I will always tell you what is in my heart. Remember that."

Paul got up and pulled her toward him, holding her close.

"Your life is your own, Gaby. I don't want to control you. I only want to protect you."

With that, he kissed her tenderly and whispered in her ear "You are in my heart."

"We'd better get back to Father and have some lunch if you want to get to San Juan for your interviews." She took his hand and they walked along the water's edge, letting their toes sink into the cool, wet sand, leaving their footprints behind them.

José had spread a blanket on the sand and had opened a bottle of white wine. He handed Paul a glass and motioned for him to take a plate. As Paul tasted the wine, Gaby filled a plate with cheese, some fruit, and slices of spicy sausage, and handed it to him along with a napkin. He sat down next to her.

"How is the water Mr. Brennan?"

"Oh, it felt great! This is a wonderful spot."

"The cove is better, huh?" José asked with a laugh, and threw a piece of bread over to him. Gaby fed her father some grapes and small pieces of bread, and poured him some wine.

"How long has Carlos owned this house?"

"Carlos bought this as a wedding present for Gabriella several years ago. A cousin of ours had worked for the seaman whose family had all perished when they tried to sail a boat to the US and drowned. Since there were no survivors, the house was available."

"But I thought that the State owned everything here in Cuba."

"Well, if you know the right people you can get what you want, Mr. Brennan. That's the way it is here."

"You mean if you are a Rojas you can get what you want," said Gaby, a bit sarcastically. José looked at her angrily, and then shook his head. He was about to say something when he looked upward and saw some dark clouds cover the sun.

"Perhaps we had better have the leftover dessert and then pack. It may rain soon." Gaby quickly cut the flan and passed the plate around. Then she began to pack the food into the basket.

"Our lovely day has almost ended," she said as she got up and moved the basket. Paul rose and helped her shake out the blanket and fold it, while José helped her father to his feet.

Gabriella took her father's arm and began to walk slowly back to the house. Paul and José followed several yards behind them, not saying much. The wind was beginning to pick up, and the sun that had scorched their backs during the morning swim now hid itself in the clouds, only occasionally deciding to come out and warm their return trip. Gaby carefully led her aging father along the sand, and as they turned away from the water into a grove of trees, he could hear her soothing voice trying to calm his fears. She turned to look in Paul's direction once, and sent him a private smile that he was to treasure forever.

As they neared the house, Gaby suddenly began to move more quickly, and Paul thought at first that her father had become ill. Soon he understood her haste. The guard and Anna were shouting and waving their arms for her to hurry, and as she ran ahead, José and Paul took each of Ricardo's arms to help him continue to walk.

By the time the three men arrived at the house, Gabriella had already gone inside. José helped his brother up the stairs, while Paul waited in the foyer. He could hear Gaby speaking quickly in Spanish. Then he heard the sound of the phone receiver being put down. She appeared nervous as she ushered him outside and away from the house.

"That was Carlos. The kidnappers want money by Wednesday, or they say they will kill his father. They have also threatened Carlos. He is sending more guards to protect us here, since he suspects that I may become a target. Paolo, he wants me to persuade you to go and help him negotiate with the kidnappers."

"*Me*! What do I know about dealing with those people? I'm only a journalist."

"Carlos thinks they will be more cooperative if an outsider deals with them. He knows how they operate. I am asking you to do this because my husband has ordered me to do it. You know I wouldn't want to send you somewhere dangerous."

"You already sent me into danger when you told me to go to Cuba, darling. I don't see how I can help. This isn't just delivering a letter."

"Carlos is not stupid. He will know the best way to handle these things. It may just involve dropping off money or a few telephone calls. Please do it for me, Paolo, so that Carlos doesn't blame me for not making you help him."

"Why can't you just tell him I refused and went to San Juan to do my job?" he protested, while his heart began to melt as he looked into her frightened eyes. Suddenly, he remembered his meeting with Mango and figured he would be sent there anyway to get closer to Carlos. Before she had time to plead anymore, he took her in his arms.

"All right, I'll go, but only if you promise to meet me when this is all over."

"Wherever you say, my darling" she murmured, as she pushed a piece of paper into his shirt pocket. "Here is the address of our house in Bogotá. Someone will meet you at the airport there." She reached up and kissed him, then whispered in his ear "vaya con Dios," but lowering her voice, added "Don't trust my husband." Hearing José and a guard coming out of the house, she pushed him away down the hill before he could ask for an explanation to her comment. "Now go and pack. The guard will drive you to San Juan. Your interviews will have to wait." She turned and ran into the house and Paul slowly made his way to the cottage.

He opened the door to find that Anna had tidied the room while he was at the beach. He glanced at his watch: 2 p.m. His meeting with Mango was set for five o'clock. He tapped out a message to his contact that he was leaving soon for SJ and that Carlos insisted he come to Bogotá. He waited for the answer. The green code numbers appeared and then the message: "Arrived SJ at noon. You are booked on a flight leaving at 6:30. Meet me executive lounge ASAP." He signed off with his code name.

Paul took a quick shower, and as he began to dress, he became anxious. He was getting into this much deeper than he wanted to, and he didn't know how to get out. Hearing a knock on the door, he opened it to see José.

"Mr. Brennan, be at the house in twenty minutes if you can."

"Thanks, José. I just have to finish packing." He closed the door and began filling the small suitcase with the few items he had taken out the day before. Raindrops began to hit the little window that Anna had left open, and he pushed it shut.

As he walked up the path to the house he could see Gabriella waiting for him. She had a black shawl over her shoulders and her long hair was covered with a dark scarf. He could visualize her praying at her mother's grave, or lighting candles at the back of the village church on Sunday. He thought that perhaps he might learn more about her by visiting her South American home, instead of this coy game-playing they were enjoying. He still wasn't sure he could trust her, and he didn't want to feel that way, but that was exactly how he felt at that moment. The guard took his suitcase and put it into the trunk. José shook his hand and he and Gaby embraced.

"Say good-bye to your father for me, Gabriella. He is a wonderful man." He turned away and slid into the back seat. As he glanced through the rearview mirror, he saw her wipe a tear from her eye and then wave good-bye. He could almost hear her silently repeating her parting refrain. The driver slowly drove down the lane and away from the old sea captain's mansion and the little cottage, and he wondered if he would ever see her again.

CHAPTER 11

Paul found his contact sitting at a tiny table in the back of the airport lounge, trying to read a newspaper in a dimly lit corner. Two empty beer bottles sat on the round table, and Paul pushed them aside and sat down.

"Greetings, Mango. So what's my next assignment?"

"Why don't you order a drink? Then bring me up to date…then listen to me."

Paul motioned for the waiter and sat down. "You sound rather serious."

"Things are getting stickier and I'm not sure you're up to this, but the department wants to take a chance on you. Actually, you're their nearest hope."

Paul ordered his drink. "Nearest hope for what?" he asked cautiously.

"Of accomplishing our objective. What can you tell me about Carlos?"

"He is definitely involved heavily in cocaine traffic, and is building a processing plant on his father-in-law's ranch, or I should say former coffee plantation. He and his father were in Cuba to negotiate a deal. Wait until you hear this—they are buying weapons and medicine from Castro to fight the anti-drug forces."

"Tell me something new, Brennan. Washington knows that Cuba has been involved in supplying the drug barons. Where is this processing plant located exactly?"

"You mean to tell me that the US has known about this information? Why are they asking me to risk my life for knowledge they already have?" Paul gulped his drink and banged his glass on the table.

"Don't get annoyed. It confirms our suspicions, and also tells us you are obtaining correct information. Did the girl tell you this?"

"Yes, and I don't know where her father's land is, by the way."

"Well, find out. When you get to Bogotá, snoop around the house and get any evidence on the Rojas operations, like invoices, letters, anything that we could use to nail him. Here is a little device which might help you." Mango handed him a tiny camera disguised as a calculator.

"Use this to copy anything you need. Here is a list of things we want to know. Memorize it and destroy it before you get on the plane. Has anyone followed you?" Mango looked around uneasily as his eyes scanned the faces coming into the lounge.

"The driver dropped me off at the departure terminal. I assume he just drove back to the house."

"Well, try to be more careful and notice anyone who seems to be tailing you. You're going into dangerous territory. Consider Cuba and your little Puerto Rican beach vacation your training. Now you'll hit the big time. State wants me to give you some courage with this gift." Mango handed him a tiny box.

"What's this?"

"Poison darts. You never know when you might need them."

"Oh come on, Mango. Isn't this a bit ridiculous?"

"No, not at all. Listen. You are new at this and you're in the big leagues now, but we have your back. Don't worry. I'll be staying close by. I'll be on the evening plane to Lima. I'll be in Bogotá by ten a.m. if I'm lucky. Then I'll contact you.

"How should I deal with these kidnappers? Carlos wants me to negotiate with them."

"Be as careful as you can. Let Carlos call the shots at first. Remember, don't let yourself become a pawn in some game. These guys can be rough on journalists. Now order another drink while I disappear. I don't want to be seen in your company for too long. By the way, did you know Bogotá is called the Athens of South America?"

Paul gave him a sidelong glance as Mango got up and walked rapidly to the door. He shoved the box into his jacket pocket and called to the waiter to order another drink to calm his nerves. What was he doing here? What would happen if he just flew back to the US and forgot all of this? Then he thought of Gaby and why he got involved in the first place. He had promised her to help Carlos. Was she to be trusted? Whose side was she on? Her whispered warning about her husband rang in his ears and he closed his eyes. As he opened them, his drink was delivered and he swigged it down. Then he heard his plane being announced. Getting up, he paid the bill and ducked into the men's room.

Finding the privacy of a stall, he opened the sheet of paper. Ten items. Places, names. They wanted to know about high-level government connections. He began to memorize them, using a code that had helped him pass high school history tests. Letters and thoughts swam in his head and when he was sure he knew it all, he tore up the note and dropped it down the toilet. They were calling his flight again. Picking up his hand luggage, he walked out just in time to see a little man in sunglasses and wild-patterned shorts staring at him through the mirror over the sink.

CHAPTER 12

Crossing over the tops of the Andes, his plane began its descent into the plateau and headed for the airport. Lights twinkled below as they flew lower and got closer to the city. Paul looked down over commercial buildings, wondering where the danger lurked and how he might avoid it. He had placed the darts in a discreet hiding place in his luggage, and his gun was strapped to his chest under his jacket. Hopefully by now, Mango was in the air on his way to Lima.

As Paul waited for his bag to arrive on the conveyer belt, he looked around for someone who might have been sent to pick him up. All he could see were women eagerly craning their necks for a husband or lover, and limo drivers holding up name cards. Grabbing his suitcase off the carousel, he put it down and dug into his pocket for the address Gaby had given him. He could call a cab and...suddenly he spotted Eduardo running frantically toward him.

"PB, thank God I didn't miss you. My brother would have killed me!" Eduardo heaved a sigh as he picked up the suitcase. Paul winced at the remark but was glad to see a familiar face.

"How are you, Eduardo?" Paul held out his hand and Eduardo shook it firmly.

"Life is more hectic than ever with this kidnapping. Carlos won't give me time off for personal business, so I have to sneak short visits in to my friends whenever I can."

"Is that why you are late? Maybe a woman?" Paul teased him.

Eduardo grinned and started to laugh.

"You know me, PB. The ladies always come first!"

"How is your father? Have you heard anything new?"

"No, nothing since this morning. Carlos is trying to raise support but is having no luck. But now that you are here, perhaps things will change." He loaded the suitcase into the trunk of the Lincoln and drove off.

"Where is the house in relation to the city?"

"About forty minutes from the center of Bogotá in a northeast suburb. You will be very comfortable there."

"How does Carlos think I can help? I have to admit I was a bit uncertain about getting involved."

"You'll have to ask Carlos, but I'm sure he has a plan. He always has a plan."

"Hmm…yes, I am sure he has one. Where are they holding your father?"

"We don't know yet, but we think not far from the city. Carlos has received two phone calls from them."

"His wife is very worried about both your father and Carlos. She told me to tell both of you to be careful."

"Gabriella has a good heart. She knows that her duty is to think about her husband's safety. I always liked her and thought Carlos chose well. She and my father have always cared for each other."

"Were you around when your family first met her?"

"Oh, yes. Everyone was gathered. A most formal occasion. She was so shy and didn't want to leave her father alone."

"It must have been a long trip for them to make from her father's ranch in Peru. How long did it take them?"

"I don't recall. I know they were quite tired when they arrived, so I guess it took many hours by truck and train and then a bus."

Eduardo switched on the radio and began to hum, so Paul decided to stop pumping him for information. They entered a residential area and the homes became more luxurious with every turn. Finally they stopped at a huge iron gate with a crest on one side and a large letter R on the other. Eduardo tapped numbers into a handheld transmitter and the gates swung open. He drove through and parked in front of a pillared entrance that was flanked by a guard on either side. A doorman appeared and opened the door for Paul while the guard helped Eduardo with the two bags. Paul walked to the front door and waited for the doorman to let him in. The foyer was full of antique Spanish artifacts. Religious statues and gold icons sat side by side every few feet down the length of the hallway, while a replica of an ancient South American Indian temple graced a round table in the center.

The doorman led him up the curved marble stairs carpeted in red velvet, and Paul let his hand glide along the carved-oak handrail, wondering how many times Gabriella's hand had touched it. At the top of the stairs, a wide hallway led to several rooms on each side. He wondered where Carlos's room was located. His room was at the very end of the hallway on the left. Perhaps the family members had rooms to the right of the stairs.

"I hope you will be comfortable here, sir," the doorman said as he flipped the light switch on and slid the bags in. Before Paul could say anything, the doorman withdrew and Eduardo came running up the stairs.

"The guest rooms are all at this end, PB. More privacy. Carlos wants us to have dinner downstairs at 9:30 so we can discuss strategy. Okay?"

"Sure. It'll just give me time to unpack and shower. See you then."

"The dining room is past the sitting room on the right." With that, Eduardo disappeared and Paul closed the door to explore the room. It was elegant, with every convenience. The drapes were drawn, but he pulled them apart and looked down into a sunken garden. Plugging in his fax, he tapped out a coded message to Mango: "Arrived R's place. Dinner at 9:30. Then on to business."

Before taking a shower, he tiptoed out into the hall to get his bearings. Walking close to the doors, he passed the curved center stairway and tried to listen for sounds. All was quiet. When he got to the end of the corridor, he could hear female voices in Spanish. Then he remembered that Carlos had a sister, and their mother of course lived in the house as well. He hurried back to the stairway and started down when he heard the front door open. He quickly sprinted back to his room and closed the door.

"So you see why I asked you to come here and help, Brennan? I can't seem to get any of father's government friends to help him."

"Why do you think they won't help, Carlos?"

"Because the sons of bitches are all self-serving hypocrites who don't deserve to live!" he screamed, while slamming his fist down on the polished table top. He buried his head in his hands, and Paul looked at Eduardo who was playfully spinning a spoon around with his index finger.

Paul tried to remember the vibrant and cocksure Carlos of the night before, in the bright mirrored dining room on the island. He was gone, and in his place, a dejected and scared little boy sat in a dark, oak-paneled, dimly lit room that couldn't hide his fear.

"Shall I clear the dishes and serve coffee here, sir?"

"No, we'll take coffee and brandy in the library, Antonetta."

Carlos raised his head and stood up. In those few moments he had been able to compose himself. Eduardo looked uneasy and suddenly turned to his brother.

"Would you mind if I not join you and PB? I promised to help Mother and Carina…."

"Don't bother to lie, Eduardo. You want to go to the city and see your whore? Then go. Just be back here tomorrow morning by 8 a.m. I may need you."

Eduardo dashed from the front room and out the front door.

"You see that my brother's priorities are not mine. They never will be. He is not serious even at this critical time."

"Perhaps that is why your father chose you to learn the business. Eduardo might be more helpful in other ways."

"What ways? He can't even protect his own ass. If he hadn't insisted on coming to Puerto Rico, my father might not have been kidnapped. He only came with me so he could visit one of his 'girlfriends' in San Juan. Let's forget about him and have our coffee."

Carlos turned to the small, glass-topped table that Antonina had just wheeled into the room, and motioned for her to pour two cups. He added some brandy to his cup and held out the bottle to Paul.

"No thanks, I'll take mine straight," he answered as he was handed his espresso.

Carlos quickly sat down. "My plan is this: I've been able to negotiate the kidnappers down to twenty million. You take two million to them tomorrow to show good faith.

"Only two?"

"Yes! You must insist on seeing and talking to my father. Until I have proof that he is alive and well, I refuse to release any more money. Call me right away. If they let me speak to him and set a date for his release, I'll have Eduardo drop off five more million. Only when I see my father set free, unharmed, will I complete the deal. This is how we have to handle things here."

"Do you really think they will work through *me*? They probably hate American journalists."

"They hate Colombian journalists more. You are an outsider. Don't worry. You'll be protected."

"I'm not sure I'm the best man for the job, Carlos. I don't speak Spanish, and I am getting worried that something will go wrong if you depend on me."

Carlos drank his brandy and then slapped Paul on the back.

"Just play by my rules and there shouldn't be any problems. Trust me. Brennan. You'll get a handsome reward."

"I'm not doing this for the money!"

Carlos looked astonished. "Then why are you helping me?"

"I don't really know. Perhaps it will make a good story for the paper. And your wife wanted me to help you. Maybe I just like adventure."

"Adventure? I liked it too until my father was kidnapped. Then I remembered that danger is part of adventure." Carlos began to ramble and slur his words, and Paul figured that he'd been drinking even before dinner.

"Maybe it's my fault, Brennan. If I had gone back with him from Havana, he probably wouldn't have been taken. I only went to see Gabriella's father because she sent me the letter begging me to come. The Santiagos are responsible for this mess!" Carlos was becoming more and more irrational and angry.

The maid interrupted him.

"Excuse me sir, but you have a call from Ramón."

Carlos stood up. "I'll take it upstairs. Well it is late, Brennan. Get some rest for tomorrow. I expect to hear from these thugs tonight, so I'll know more in the morning. See you at breakfast, say seven?"

"Fine. Goodnight. Sleep well, Carlos."

He left the room to take the call. Paul felt for his little camera hidden deep in his right pocket, and pulled it out. Slowly closing the library doors, he swiftly turned and reached the desk in the back corner. The center drawer was unlocked, but he only found some pencils, ink, paper, and a letter opener. The top of the desk was littered with pink message forms with scribbled phone numbers, addresses, and Spanish words he couldn't read. Unopened letters were jammed into the gold wire stand and a stack of official-looking, typewritten pages were piled at the right corner. The seal told him they were Cuban documents, so he didn't bother looking at them. He tugged at a drawer that seemed stuck. He gave up and tried the one beneath it. Pulling it slowly toward him he spied a thick leather ledger and pulled it out. Placing it on the desk, he opened the cover and turned the pages rapidly, noticing the dates and quantities of items. He aimed his camera on a few pages and quickly snapped some photos. Suddenly he heard the phone beep. Carlos had hung up. He had to finish soon. He closed the ledger and put it back into the drawer. Then he opened the bottom drawer and removed an appointment book. Checking the March entries, he spotted a meeting with a Jorge Bosa on the fourth and again on the twelfth. That was the day before Gaby's brother was killed! He took a few more pictures and flipped through the April listings, the month Carlos supposedly bought his father-in-law's ranch. Replacing the appointment book, he glanced at the addresses on the envelopes in the rack. San Juan, Havana, Cartagena, Lima...then he saw one addressed to José Santiago, Number 16 Avenue des Angeles. He opened the envelope to see some kind of letter to Gaby's uncle with a list and some addresses. How he wished he had learned to read Spanish better!

Just then his eye caught a beam of light under the door coming from the hallway. He held his breath and edged away from the desk toward the couch. Then the light went out and he heard no footsteps. Should he continue searching? All of a sudden, the phone rang! He walked briskly over to the desk and silently released the receiver from its cradle after it had stopped ringing. He listened while Carlos spoke in rapid Spanish. Hearing the name "Paolo," his gripped tightened around the phone. Her voice was unmistakable. It was Gaby. Why was she calling here? Had something happened to her father? The conversation ended without her familiar closing. Perhaps that is **their** special message, Paul thought, and he smiled as he hung up and walked to the library door. Enough snooping, he thought. Opening the door, he peeked out. No one was around. He slowly began to climb the stairs hoping no one was watching him.

"*Buenos noches*, señor."

Hearing a female voice, he looked up and saw a dark-haired teenager leaning over the railing waving her arms.

"Hello. You must be Carlos's sister."

"Yes, I am Carina." She proceeded to follow him along the hallway, her youthful figure draped in a silky black peignoir that floated to the floor behind her.

"You are Mr. Brennan, no?"

"Yes, that's right. She began to play with her long dark hair, moving her arms suggestively.

"Shouldn't you be in bed? It's late, Miss Rojas.

"Oh no. Mother let's me stay up as long as I want. Would you like to talk to me?"

"No, I'm tired. I don't think your brother would like to see you dressed like that talking to a guest. Let's talk tomorrow at breakfast."

Paul quickly closed his bedroom door, shutting out the spoiled, young temptress.

After checking the fax, he tapped a code to Mango. "Shot some pics. Tomorrow meeting kidnappers...address for JS 16 Avenue des Angeles, Lima. Read?" After a few seconds, he heard a beep. "Be careful. I'll be close by."

Paul dialed off and went to sleep.

CHAPTER 13

"Now remember, Brennan: the deal is off if my father is not released by Wednesday morning."

"Understood. Don't worry, Carlos. I'll do my best for you." With that Paul climbed into the back seat of the grey limo next to the briefcase full of thousand dollar bills. Eduardo leaned on the accelerator and they were off.

The drop-off point was south of the city, near an abandoned cement factory. Paul had hidden the darts in little pockets sewn into his shoes. The pen in the secret compartment of his jacket pocket was the shooter, and the Glock handgun was strapped snugly under his left arm. Beads of sweat dropped off his forehead when they neared the spot, and he pulled his handkerchief out to wipe his face. As they waited, he could hear his heart beat out a song of fear. Eduardo smoked a cigarette and appeared to be impatient to leave. Train whistles suddenly blew nearby.

"This area was once a vibrant industrial center that shipped goods all over South America." Paul looked outside the window and saw weeds choking the black, tarred road, breaking it into jagged pieces whose mud-filled cracks held broken glass and debris from an earlier, happier time. Eduardo glanced in the rearview mirror.

"This is the pick-up car. You can get out."

Paul grabbed the briefcase, opened the back door and got out. Before he was able to close the door, Eduardo revved the engine and Paul slammed the door shut. With a quick wave he was gone, and Paul was alone, following the kidnappers' orders. The black van screeched to a halt and two men in masks jumped out and surrounded him. Pushing him toward the van, they trained their guns on him.

"Open the case!"

One of them checked the suitcase while the other one threw Paul into the back of the van and blindfolded him. Locking the back doors, they took off. Paul tried to count to estimate how far the drop-off point was to the hideaway. The van surged and lurched and crossed a railroad track. Then it abruptly stopped. The doors opened and he was pushed out and led forward. He climbed ten steps and followed a walkway, going through a door. Someone tugged at his blindfold and suddenly he could see after his eyes became accustomed to the light.

He was in some kind of warehouse with boxes and crates filling a long narrow room. Shafts of light from dirty side windows illuminated the dust, and wood shavings littered the dirt floor.

"Where is Señor Rojas?"

A voice behind him cackled a hellish laugh, and he turned to see a bearded, fierce-looking guerilla in battle fatigues.

"He is with the rats in the basement."

"I was told to speak to him to verify that he is alive and well."

"Oh, he is alive all right."

"Is there a phone here? His son must speak to him before you get the next payment."

The bearded guerilla came toward Paul pointing his gun at him. "You do not dictate to me, American. Carlos Rojas will have to sweat some more before he sees his father. Jorge, frisk him. Then take him to see Rojas."

"Look, I came to negotiate, not to be bullied."

"Shut up you American bastard." He pointed the gun at Paul's head while one of the soldiers checked him, removing his gun.

"What do you think you'll do with that, American?" He threw the gun across the floor, then motioned for Paul to be taken downstairs. Shoving him down the dark steps in front of him, the guard yelled out "A visitor for you, señor!" Paul heard soft moaning.

"You have five minutes!" the guard announced before walking back up the stairs and closing the door.

Paul looked around, trying to see where Carlos's father might be. He smelled foul odors, and dampness pervaded the stale, dank air as he walked slowly toward the sounds.

"Señor Rojas, where are you? Carlos sent me."

The moans grew louder until Paul found him curled in a corner, his hands tied with rope, his bearded face red and swollen. Paul bent down to speak to him.

"My name is Brennan. Paul Brennan. I am an American journalist. I came here with money from your son to get you out. Do you understand me?"

Carlos's father took a few shallow breaths and tried to speak.

"Carlos, *dónde* Carlos?"

"He is in Bogotá, at your house. He is fine. He sent two million dollars and wants me to negotiate for him. If I can get word to him, the kidnappers will release you."

"They are barbarians!" he screamed.

"Can you stand? I need to know your condition before I telephone your son."

"I...don't...know...how long have I been here?"

"It is Monday morning, and I believe you were kidnapped on Saturday."

"Oh yes, I remember now. But you cannot escape from here."

"No, you don't understand. They will let us leave."

Suddenly a booming voice echoed through the basement, and he turned to see the guerilla on the stairs. "It is you who do not understand, Mr. Brennan. Do you think I am stupid?"

"No, just a cruel, evil, no-good SOB," Paul murmured to himself. "This man is hurt. He needs to be released to a hospital. Where is the phone?"

"There is no phone here."

"I need to speak to Carlos so that you can receive the other payments."

"Don't give these hoodlums a cent!" shouted Jorge Rojas, rubbing the bump on his head, leaning against the wall for support while he tried to stand.

"Shut up, old man!" The guerilla hit Rojas and he fell to the ground.

"Look, be reasonable. Unless you cooperate you won't get any more money from his son. Isn't that what you want?"

"We want assurances from this old man that he will influence convention delegates so that our candidate will win the next election. We also want him to give up his private claim to oil reserves on his land. Otherwise, his son will get a bullet between his eyes."

Paul looked at Rojas, a cringing mass of nerves on a rat-infested, dirty floor, pulling at his ropes and moaning in pain. He struggled and then threw down his arms in defeat. He nodded yes and mumbled "All right, I will do it." Paul helped him up. The soldier motioned for Paul to go up the stairs. When they got to the top, he pushed Paul ahead of him and out the door.

"The phone is in the van. We will call Carlos and arrange a pickup." Paul walked out of the warehouse and over to the van and climbed into the front passenger seat. The driver handed him a phone. He frantically dialed the number.

"Carlos. It's PB. He's all right. He's been beaten but he can speak and stand on his own. I think they are ready to settle. He told them what they wanted to hear." The guerilla tore the phone away from Paul and spoke to Carlos in Spanish. Then he hung up and they went back inside. Paul heard Rojas being escorted up the basement stairs and he felt relieved.

"Carlos will drop off more money in a few hours. We will pick it up. Only then will we finalize things." The guerilla sat down on the floor and smashed a beer bottle against a metal box, holding it up to Paul as if toasting him. He drank greedily from the broken edge, then tossed the bottle aside.

"Carlos must have his father by Wednesday morning, or the deal is off," Paul announced. "He also insists on speaking to his father."

"The deal is off when I *say* it is off!" he screamed. Paul shuddered and looked around for his gun.

Suddenly the bearded guerilla came toward him, mesmerized by something he saw. Paul stood up but the man grabbed his arm and tore the pager from his wrist.

"This thing is interesting…I think I will like this." He strapped it onto his own wrist and began to play with the numbers.

"It's useless to you unless you know the codes!" Paul shouted, feeling suddenly naked and exposed without his lifeline to Mango.

The guerilla began to laugh again. "It is more useless to you if it is on my wrist!" he proclaimed, strutting around to show it off to his men.

The warm stifling air of the warehouse became oppressive, and Paul swirled the warm beer around in his parched mouth. He was becoming a bit dizzy from not having had lunch when he heard the van leave to pick up the money. He passed the time thinking about Gabriella as she looked on the beach, wringing out her wet hair. Where was Mango? He was supposed to be watching over him. If only he could send him a message.

Rojas had fainted once, but was now resting against a box. Paul was not allowed to sit near him or talk to him. The guerillas were probably as bored as he was. Paul closed his eyes and tried to rest. Hearing voices, he looked up. Jorge and the bearded loudmouth were back with another suitcase full of bills. They gloated about their success, patting each other on the back and speaking in a quick, clipped manner, pushing and shoving each other playfully.

"Get Rojas in the van, Jorge," the bearded guerilla commanded.

Paul got up to help, but they shoved him aside. He began to follow them, but Jorge took a gun and held it to his chin.

"You're not going anywhere, American!" Then the bearded man pushed him down with his foot. Paul got up, ready to fight. Jorge jumped him from behind and the guerilla smashed his fist into Paul's face and punched him in the stomach.

"Tie him up. We'll be back soon." Paul began to feel punches and slaps and a rifle butt strike his skull. Then everything went black.

CHAPTER 14

Mango sent a second message on his pager and waited. He got no reply.

"Damn," he shouted, then lit a Cuban cigar and puffed nervously. He looked up at the Rojas mansion from across the street and wondered what had happened.

"Where the hell are you Brennan?" he thought. Four hours and no sign of him.

Screeching tires jolted him upright in the seat of his car, and he pulled his gun out of its holster. A large, shiny grey limo pulled up to the back entrance and Carlos emerged and opened the back door. His brother quickly ran around to help Carlos carry the elder Rojas into the house.

"I don't like this," Mango whispered to himself. "Why isn't Brennan with them?

He watched as the two brothers struggled to lift and carry the old gentleman, who was clearly not able to walk on his own.

****

The rocking and jarring of the van, rumbling along the rough, unpaved road, made the pounding in his head worse, and Paul slowly awoke and carefully opened his eyes. The smell of beer invaded his nostrils as he tried to focus his vision from his position on the floor in the middle of the vehicle. The guerilla who was guarding him was obviously having a difficult time staying awake. Sitting crossed-legged near the door, his head bobbed from side to side with each sway of the van. His gun lay next to him but almost out of reach, having been slowly shaken away from him by the van's movement. Bottles littered the area near the back door and the guerilla held a beer in his hand, taking a drink now and then. Where were they taking him, he wondered?

Paul decided to inch his way toward the darker recesses of the van, in order to work on the ropes around his wrist which were not tied very tightly. Carefully he bent his legs just enough to push backward, silently moving into the shadows. Rubbing his wrists back and forth, he was able to loosen his shackles a bit until they came free. Feeling for his shooter, he pulled it out and opened it. Gingerly reaching down to his shoe, he retrieved two darts and loaded one into the shooter. Now all he had to do was to work his way back close enough to aim, and wait for the right moment.

All of a sudden, the van swerved and the guerilla rallied, shouting something in Spanish and waving his arms wildly. He slowly raised the bottle to his lips, and as he threw his head back to pour the beer down his throat, Paul saw his chance. Placing the shooter to his lips and taking aim, he sent a dart down toward the guerilla's outstretched neck. He slumped forward and dropped the bottle which rolled toward Paul, who crawled over to check the guerilla's pulse. When he was sure that he was dead, he looked out of the back window. It was dark outside. Fumbling, he picked up the gun and waited until the van slowed. Pushing the door open, he crouched down and jumped, rolling to the side of the road and into the cover of some thick bushes. As he waited in the darkness, holding his breath, he heard the van continue on without slowing down, the driver apparently unaware he had lost precious cargo. He rested for a bit, and then stood up slowly to make sure there were no broken limbs. He began to walk in the same direction the van had taken, since he had no idea where they had meant to deliver him. He saw a sign for Medellín, and soon heard the sound of a truck engine. Looking down the road behind him, he saw an old pickup lumbering toward him. He decided to stand in the middle of the road and wave his hands, pointing toward the town.

The farmer slowed and braked, motioning him to jump in the back. Paul joined the vegetable crates and they took off. He leaned back against a box of oca tubers after removing one pinkish-red one. Chewing the top off, he tried to formulate his game plan. He would need to quickly get out of sight in the next town, where his former captors were certainly headed; they would notice his absence as soon as they arrived at their destination. Where could he go? Back to

Bogotá? How would he get there? He had no money and no ID. Where would Mango look for him? He decided to try to find the nearest newspaper office. He might be able to get a message out to his paper or to Mango.

The truck slowed, and he gazed out at the poor suburbs wallowing in filth and hopelessness. Broken boards tried to hide the squalor from the road, but he could see roofs that needed repair, outdoor toilets with hardly any cover from the elements, and rusted trucks and cars littering backyards. Roosters began to crow, and some industrious women were already scrubbing rags in a large tin washtub outside their doors.

The truck almost slowed to a crawl, and he turned to the left to see groups of women and priests walking by, as if in a trance. Women with thick white makeup smeared on their gaunt faces walked straight ahead, their sad, downcast eyes telling the story. Gloved fingers grasped burning candles and veiled heads moaned and uttered mournful tones. Some of them held signs, and Paul recognized the word for drugs.

The truck pushed its way beyond the crowd and sped up. As it neared the town the driver shouted something to Paul, and he saw a sign announcing the city: Medellín. So this is where they were taking him! Paul jumped off the truck and waved thanks to the driver, who shouted something in Spanish and drove off. Paul began to make his way toward the center of this huge city.

The dawn had broken as he walked past storefronts with bins full of fruit and windows revealing meat hanging from hooks. A little boy pushed his swollen, dirty face against the glass, eyeing the food. Paul recognized the distended belly and the malnourished leg bones he had seen on his Romanian assignment. Seeing Paul, he held out his hands and grasped Paul's leg, sobbing in Spanish. Paul crouched down and put his arms around the boy, trying to comfort him. Little did the kid know that Paul had no more money than he did at that moment, and neither one of them could afford a banana or a piece of beef.

"I'm hungry too, little one," Paul murmured, as he moved on, leaving him to his private hell. He needed to find that office. Then he had an idea. Running back to the boy, he repeated the name of a paper he knew that operated out of Medellín. He pointed to the newspaper rack sitting outside the door of the grocery shop. The boy's eyes suddenly brightened, and somehow he understood that Paul wanted to be taken there. He took Paul's hand and began to walk across the street and then down alleys, past larger streets and across a little park. They walked along quickly, not stopping to peek at the orchid greenhouse or the ornate church whose open doors invited the faithful to enter, to try and forget the hatred in the streets. The boy suddenly stopped and pointed to a row of buildings across the street. They crossed and went up to the gate. It was locked tight.

"Que hora?" Paul asked the boy, looking at his imaginary watch while pointing to the office. The boy held up seven fingers. So they opened at 7 a.m. Paul patted his head, wondering what time it was now.

Church bells began to ring before he had a chance to ask his little friend the time. He thought it was strange that parishioners would be called to service on a weekday so early. Then the crowds he had passed while in the truck filled the square and started to sing. The women wept and the priests made speeches. The little boy ran across and joined one of the girls he obviously knew. Perhaps it was his sister or mother. Paul crossed the street and began to mix with the crowd, thinking it might be a good way to avoid being spotted by the guerillas. Tear-stained faces sobbed pitifully, holding framed photos of their loved ones who had probably been killed or had died using drugs. The group began to move toward the church and Paul went along with them, pretending to be part of the protest.

Once inside, he drifted to the back so he could stay near the door. After the hymn, he turned and started to walk outside. Spotting a military truck driving slowly along the boulevard near the square, he ducked back inside the church and sat down. He began to listen to the priest, deciding to leave when the group did. He rested and closed his eyes, letting the chants and prayers and Latin intonations lull him into a soft, spiritual repose. He thought again of Gaby and longed to be near her. If only he had money, he would buy her an orchid from the greenhouse or from a flower shop. He could imagine her smile as she gently held the flower or placed it in her hair. Going back to Bogotá and trying to make contact with Mango was the only wise decision. He opened his eyes when footsteps began to echo, and he got up and joined the throngs, slowly threading his way to the door.

He quickly sprinted across the park and entered through the now-open gate of the newspaper office, trying to explain his dilemma to the guard. Finally he was escorted to the lobby and waited until someone from the overseas desk who spoke English could see him.

A pretty secretary handed him a cup of hot coffee and told him to wait until she found someone who handled US news. Finally he was shown into someone's office.

"Hello. I am Señor Cortez. Sorry to have kept you waiting, but I was in an emergency meeting." Paul thrust out his hand to shake.

"Nice to meet you. Paul Brennan from the *New York World*. Don't apologize."

"How can I help you?"

"I need to get a message to my paper or to my contact. I was kidnapped by a group who had taken Jorge Rojas prisoner, after I helped arrange for his release. I was able to get free of them but I am sure they are looking for me. I had to kill one of them."

"We are in a dangerous profession here in South America, Mr. Brennan. Where do you want to go?"

"I need to return to Bogotá as soon as I can."

"I have a reporter leaving for that city in a few hours. You could ride with him if you like. Until then, you can get some sleep in the lounge down the hall. It isn't fancy, but there is a couch. Just keep out of sight. I don't want any trouble with traffickers."

"I don't want to cause you any more problems. But can I trouble you for some food? I haven't eaten since yesterday morning."

"Sure. Marguerita will show you where you can get some rolls and more coffee. I'll wake you at noon for the ride."

"Do you think you can get word to my paper that I am safe and will return to Bogotá today? They may be able to contact someone who I'm sure is looking for me."

"Of course. Give me a name to contact and I'll try to send a message."

"I don't know how to thank you. I will repay the kindness when I return to the States. What can I do for you?"

"Just tell the world what you are seeing here in Colombia. That will be payment enough. Now get some sleep."

Paul gorged on yellow cheese bread rolls, slipping a few into his pocket for later. He gulped down mouthfuls of hot, dark coffee and then curled up on the worn sofa in a dingy corner near a copier and drifted off to a fitful sleep, hoping his savior could be trusted.

CHAPTER 15

Mango grabbed his luggage off the conveyer belt and walked out the door of the airport in Lima. Giving the taxi driver José's address, he lit a cigar and settled into the back seat while they drove downtown. Mango stared out at the shanty towns they were passing, suddenly remembering his past. His best friend had lived in a leaky oil drum, and his own home had been built of cardboard pieces attached to the remnants of a stucco structure, apparently destroyed shortly before his family found and claimed it as theirs. They were told that the occupants had died in the house and that the authorities could find no relatives who wanted to move in. Row upon row of *"pueblos jovenes"* or young towns, had sprung up here, inhabited by destitute Peruvians in search of a better life in the city. He puffed his Cuban cigar and closed the window, shutting out the smell of his past. Well, they could all better themselves as he had done, he told himself. Don't feel sorry for them. If they work hard, they can make it.

The taxi stopped at a traffic light and a group of beggars surrounded the car. As Mango turned to look into youthful faces hardened by despair, he laughed at what he had just been thinking. Only one in a million of those poor bastards will ever "make it" he thought to himself. They are all doomed to live out their lives in poverty, and there was not a thing he could do about it.

The taxi pulled up to a modest house in a neighborhood not far from the beach resort of Miraflores. Mango jumped out and paid the driver, taking his small bag and telling him to wait. He walked up the small path bordered by flower beds and knocked on the door. No answer. Then he spotted someone peeking out of the thin, limp curtain stretched across one small window near the door. He waited. The door slowly opened, and a boy around twelve peered out and asked his name.

"I am looking for José Santiago. Do you know where he is?"

"My uncle is not here. Has he done something wrong?"

"No. I am looking for a friend of his—an American. Have you seen any Americans lately?"

Suddenly Mango heard a woman's voice from inside the house behind the boy.

"Go upstairs, Tomás. I will speak to the man. What do you want with my husband?" she said suspiciously.

"My name is Antonio Cenera. I am looking for a friend of your husband's. His name is Paul Brennan. He was with your husband in Cuba last week and has disappeared. He was staying with your niece's husband, Carlos Rojas."

"I know nothing about my husband's business with the Rojas family. I haven't seen José in a month."

"Have you heard from him at all since he left Lima?"

Before she could answer, the boy, who had been listening to the conversation, whispered something to her.

"My nephew says he saw your friend when he was in the Caribbean, and that Mr. Brennan helped his sister Gabriella. But I have not spoken with my husband for awhile. I cannot help you."

"If he comes here, tell him to get in touch with me. It is urgent." Mango pulled out a business card and gave it to her, then turned and walked back to the waiting taxi and got in.

"Drive down the street, out of sight, and let me out. Wait for me there." He thrust some American bills into the driver's hand and jumped out. He walked back and watched the house for nearly an hour. Then he gave up and climbed into the back seat of the taxi. Turning his pager on, he tapped a code and then the message: Reporting lost watch.... Last contact Sunday night from Bogotá.... Lima checked negative. Need instructions. He waited for a moment. Then the pager beeped. Message: Go back to base point Bogotá tomorrow and continue hunt. Mango hung up and told the driver to go back to the airport. Looking out the window again at the dirty slums, comparing them to the clean, neat, trim little Santiago home, Mrs. Santiago's words came back to him. He wondered how much she knew about her husband's dealings with the Rojas family.

CHAPTER 16

Gaby and Paul followed the leafy wooded path on horseback, with the gentle clip clop of the horses' hooves accompanying her soft laughter. Tropical palm fronds brushed their legs and as she turned a corner, he suddenly lost sight of her. Noisy mechanical sounds blended with the wind's roar and he yelled her name.

"Wake up, Mr. Brennan. It is time to leave."

His eyes reluctantly opened to see Marguerita, the secretary at the news office. Journalists were rushing about and he could hear a variety of office noises, no longer a part of his dream.

"Here is the man who will take you to Bogotá."

Paul stood up and saw a thin man about his age, holding a notebook with sunglasses perched on top of his black hair. They exchanged greetings.

"Nice to know you, Luis. And thanks for doing this for me."

"We'll go out the back way so you won't be noticed. Get into the back seat and stay on the floor until we get out of the city."

"Is that really necessary?"

"Yes, it is. We have already had two journalists killed for covering stories about the cartel, and several bombs have been planted. If you were kidnapped by a guerilla group, they may be headquartered near here and will be looking for you."

Paul climbed onto the floor of the back seat and Luis threw a blanket over him. After Luis showed his press ID, Paul could hear the car being waved through the exit gate.

"We are taking some alleys to avoid the main road, but soon I will have to drive for a few blocks on the boulevard to get to the highway. Sit tight. We should get through this okay." Luis maneuvered the car deftly and quickly, making abrupt turns and slowing only if he encountered traffic lights.

"Have you worked in Medellín long?" Paul asked from under his covering.

"About a year. I was working in Miami when a promotion came up here. I took it for a change of scenery and for better bucks. Then I met a girl and married her. You know the story. Now she won't leave her family to go back to the US with me. But sometime soon we may have to get out of this..." All of a sudden, Luis applied the brakes and Paul felt the car slow and heard screeching noises.

"What's happening, Luis?"

Shots rang out and Paul heard bullets hitting the windshield. The car began to swerve as if out of control. Paul had to see what was happening. Whipping off the blanket, he got up to look. Luis tried to grip the wheel as he fell over on the passenger seat, blood spurting from his mouth and forehead. Paul reached over and took the wheel, turning it out of the path of a truck coming toward them. Luckily Luis had braked and thrown the clutch into neutral. As it slowed, Paul jumped over the seat and sat on Luis's legs so he could reach the pedals. Looking quickly at the rearview mirror, he saw several bodies lying in the road and some people were running away. A white car barreled down the street behind them in the opposite direction.

Paul panicked. Luis's eyes stared up at him and he knew he was dead. He opened the driver's door and got out. Pulling Luis by his legs, he left him on the side of the road and jumped into the driver's seat. He had to get out of there quickly and find the highway that would take him to Bogotá. There was no map in the glove compartment. Reaching for the blanket, he covered the bloodstained seat next to him and drove off, anxious to get away before the police arrived.

He turned on the radio and listened to some music to try to calm down. Sweat rolled off his face as he imagined Luis's wife hearing about his death. He had only known the reporter for ten minutes, but feelings of guilt swept over him, as if he had something to do with the man's killing. Did he? Were these killers the same beasts who had kidnapped him? He pushed that thought out of his head. He promised to do something nice for that family when this was all behind him.

He searched for road signs but saw no sign of the name of the city. Then he recognized the little grocery store where he had met the boy. He must be on the road the kidnappers followed! After a mile or so, a large, blue sign announced that he was going in the right direction toward the city. He began to breathe a bit easier, and pressed the accelerator to the floor, checking the gas gauge. He had a full tank, thank God. He didn't want to stop for anything, even lunch. He pulled the stale rolls from his pocket and chewed the dry bread. Then he started thinking about Mango and wondered where he might be. If only he had his pager, he thought. Mango must be frantic. Perhaps now he would know that Paul was safe if the Medellín paper had gotten through to New York, and if the message had been sent on to officials in DC. He drove on, up and down hills, trying to piece all of it together.

How much did Carlos have to do with his kidnapping? Had he tried to rescue him? These questions only made him more nervous, and he opened the window for some fresh air. He had to find Mango soon and tell him he wanted *out*. He was no good at it. Starving children and sobbing widows crowded his thoughts, and he wondered if the US drug war was helping these people. If they wanted them to stop growing their coca beans they had better offer a substitute just as lucrative.

On and on he drove, trying to think clearly while putting miles behind him. How did Gaby figure into all this? He still didn't know if she was as innocent as she claimed. Trying to sort out his feelings for her, he listened to upbeat Latin rhythms on the radio, thinking about everything she had told him from the beginning. It was true she had lied, but perhaps she had no other way out. Carlos must be hell to live with. He tried to analyze her but kept hitting a brick wall. When a lovely, sad ballad began to play, a strange, warm feeling came over him, and he suddenly felt calm. It was as if a sweet, fragrant air had wafted in through the window, telling him how he felt about her. For the first time, he understood that he loved her. He was finally thinking clearly. An overwhelming feeling of joy and solicitude replaced fear and doubt about her. He needed to protect her, and he wanted her to need him.

A news report suddenly broke his reverie, and he tried to translate but couldn't understand the words. Then he heard the name. Luis Cruzan. Medellín. He recognized the name of the newspaper. They must have found the body.

Paul was approaching the outskirts of Bogotá. He headed downtown toward the hotel where he figured Mango was probably staying. He parked the car a few blocks away in a vacant lot and walked into the lobby. After getting the room number from the desk clerk he dialed the house phone.

"Brennan! Where the hell have you been? I just filed a missing contact report with headquarters."

"I'm no longer missing. I'll come right up and tell you all about it."

"You look horrible!" shouted Mango as he closed the door. "Go take a shower while I send your clothes out to be cleaned and pressed. I'll order dinner and you can bring me up to date."

"Thanks. You have no idea what I've been through."

"Oh yes I do. I've been at this a long time."

"By the way, I left a car a few blocks away. Better get rid of it. There are blood stains on the front seat."

Mango took Paul's clothes and picked up the phone, while Paul settled into a hot steamy shower, already tasting the juicy steak he heard Mango order.

■■

"It sounds like the M19 group did the kidnapping," Mango thought aloud as he swirled the golden cognac in his glass. "They aren't as disciplined as some other guerilla outfits."

"If they had been, I probably wouldn't be here enjoying this steak!"

"What other details can you remember about the guerilla band?"

"When I first met Rojas in the basement, they insisted that he promise to influence delegates before they would let him go."

"The National Assembly convenes next year to rewrite the constitution. Drug barons want to make sure they won't be extradited to the US."

"But what can Rojas do?"

"He has many influential friends who are delegates. He himself is an alternate and might find himself in a position to vote. What else?"

"They also wanted him to give up rights to some oil-rich land he apparently owns. They held Rojas in some kind of warehouse outside of town. I'd say about twenty minutes by car. I don't remember the leader's name, but his sidekick was named Jorge. I think I've told you all that I can remember right now, Mango."

"Well, if you think of something later, be sure to tell me. It may be important."

"I still feel terrible about Luis and the kid who helped me to find the newspaper office."

"Look Brennan. Stop feeling guilty. It'll interfere with your work. Don't you understand that Carlos doesn't give a damn about you? He traded you for his father, pure and simple. He didn't try to rescue you and probably doesn't want to deal with you anymore. He used you. As for the kid who helped you...he may have tipped off the kidnappers who may have been the ones who ambushed the car. Kids here will do anything for money or food."

"Mango, I want out of this mess. I tried to help, but I'm no good at this. I'm tired of kidnappers, dead bodies, and killing. I keep seeing myself mutilated and trapped. I've had enough! I am a reporter and want to go back to reporting. Just reporting!"

"You can't get out that easily, PB. You must go back to the Rojas house and get the film you took. We need hard evidence. I've been working on a theory that José Santiago is more involved than we realized. Your pictures might prove that."

"How can I go back to Carlos's house if they suspect that I am working for my government?"

"Well, they might have known that all along. Intelligence tells me that both Rojas sons are spending most of their time at the hospital protecting their father. Where did you put the film?"

"I was afraid to take it with me to the meeting with the kidnappers, so I hid it in my room."

"You've got to gain entrance to the house long enough to retrieve it. If you get it to me, I'll tell the State Department that you want out. Who can you use to help you get into the house?"

"Perhaps the maid will let me...wait a minute. The daughter was coming on to me a lot the night before I left."

"Perfect. Use her."

"I don't know, Mango. Carlos is pretty protective of his family and she's only a teenager."

"Do you remember that you owe me one for getting back Gabriella's note to her father?"

"And you promised to do something about her brother...the one who lives in the sewers."

"Now don't tell me you still have feelings for that woman after what her husband did to you!"

"I think I'm in love with her. I need her. I need to help her family. I promised her that."

"You can help her more by not quitting on me. Don't you understand that her country needs to verify their cooperation in the drug war in order to receive US aid? There's a good chance that Washington might cut them off if things don't improve. Congress may decide to cancel any agreements they made. Four million malnourished Colombians need you to fight."

"That's just my point. From what I've seen, I don't think burning coca plant fields and causing unrest is helping these people."

"Look, PB. The State Department and the White House really don't care what you think. They only want results. You'll have to wait until we can find a replacement for you. And forget Carlos's wife. The US isn't absolutely sure what side she's on. It could be very dangerous for you if you feel this way about her. I also have an obligation to report this relationship to headquarters. They won't be happy about it."

"I don't care. Our government promised to help her brother if I got involved. I almost lost my life for them. The least they could do is…"

Mango interrupted him. "All right. I think I may have found her brother. We can go downtown later tonight and try to persuade him to come with us. But I doubt if we can get him to give up his life underneath the city."

"I want to try."

"Get a few hours' sleep. Then I'll wake you and we will go and see the kid, if you promise to go back to the Rojas home. Tell them you just came to collect your things. Play dumb, like you thought they tried their best to free you. But get that film and get back here. I'll give you until noon tomorrow. If you're not back by then, the team will try and rescue you."

"This is my last mission, Mango. When it's over I want nothing more to do with the State Department. I'm out, understand?"

"Of course…you pay me back for the note and we're even. I'll wake you around nine."

Paul's head hit the pillow and he was out fast, quickly resuming his dream of galloping on horseback along the water's edge with Gaby.

CHAPTER 17

The downtown streets swarmed with fast moving cars and pedestrians trying to push their way through the crowded sidewalks. Elegant women stepped out of black limos with their noses tilted at an upward angle. They sent forth subtle clouds of jasmine, as Paul and Mango followed along behind them like obedient dogs tracking a scent. Dripping with jewels and clutching their fur stoles, they clicked their high heels across the pavement, following their partners to the entrance of posh clubs. Further along, the neighborhood began to deteriorate, and the faces changed with the scenery. Poor, thin youths sold drugs at curbside, and hollow-cheeked addicts wandered by, their glazed eyes searching the ground for answers.

"Not so fast, Mango. I can't keep up with you."

"We're almost there. I need to find this priest who knows the kids."

The evening lights of the shops and bars behind them lit up the sky, trying in vain to hide the city's shame by dressing her in flashy colors and shapes. Paul followed Mango down an alley and into the side door of a church.

"Father Davila!" Mango yelled as he spotted the cleric rising from his knees in front of the altar. The young priest turned around and greeted Mango.

"It is good to see you, Antonio."

"This is the friend who wanted to look for someone in the sewers, Father. Paul Brennan."

The priest held out his hand and shook Paul's. "It is not often that I meet someone with such a request, Mr. Brennan. Who are you looking for?"

"A boy by the name of Manuel Santiago. A Peruvian. He came here at least six months ago. He should be about sixteen."

"Why do you want to see him?"

"I promised his sister I would try to find him."

"Forgive the questions, Mr. Brennan. Many local authorities are hunting these poor children and sometimes even killing them. I am only trying to protect them."

"You can trust Mr. Brennan, Father. He is an American journalist helping the DEA. Can you take us down tonight?"

"To the sewers? Of course. I go there every night with food and blankets. I would be pleased to show someone new our underground population. Wait here. I will only be a moment."

Father Davila disappeared, and Mango suddenly crossed himself and walked over to the rack of candles, lighting one and dropping some money into a little wooden box.

"That man is a saint, Brennan. He goes to the sewers every night."

"Mango, I thought you told me you had already found Manuel."

"I tracked the priest down and started investigating. I've also spoken to the police and they seem to remember someone by that name who was picked up for stealing last month."

A side door squeaked open and the priest returned carrying boxes and bags.

"Would each one of you take two items please, and follow me?"

Father Davila opened the back door and they followed him down the alley. After making a few turns, he walked to the center of the street and dropped to his knees. He knocked four times on the metal plate covering the sewer entrance, the sound reverberating down the dark, dank alley. They waited. Then suddenly the lid popped open—a smiling face appeared, and an arm reached up to take a bag and welcome the priest. Father Davila spoke to the boy in Spanish, then called Mango and Paul to come down. He and Mango groped their way gingerly down the narrow, circular metal stairs to the bottom, trying to keep their balance as they handed the boxes down to Father Davila.

"This is my helper, Raymondo," the priest told them. "He keeps me informed and helps me distribute things."

Following the boy and the priest, Mango and Paul walked along a narrow corridor, lit only by an occasional match or kerosene lamp. The foul odor was almost unbearable, and Paul began to cough. Pulling his handkerchief from his pocket, he covered his mouth as they continued on, hearing the drip of condensation from pipes overhead. Paul's shoes became covered in grimy sludge, and their footsteps echoed in this chamber of hell as they trudged on, not knowing their destination.

The corridor soon led into a larger room, and Paul's eyes fell on thirty or forty children huddled on the floor trying to get comfortable for the night. The lucky few who had spots on wall ledges stretched out, and he spotted a teenage girl, obviously pregnant, lying on her side with her head cradled in a young boy's lap. The priest looked up at her and shook his finger.

"Maria, you must come up and stay with the nuns soon. You promised." He then began tossing small bags of food toward the group, and the boys began to catch them, tearing them open and devouring the morsels.

"These kids probably haven't eaten since yesterday when I was here," the priest said in a low voice. Then he pulled Raymondo over and handed him some blankets to give out. Mango began to speak to the boy in Spanish and Paul looked away, feeling bitter and saddened to see such horror. In a corner, a rat fed on some sewage and a sickly child held out a feeble hand to the priest, begging for something to drink. The child's eyes burned with fever and the priest wrapped him in a blanket.

"That child will not last the night," he confided to Paul, who suddenly felt overwhelmed with disgust.

"Isn't there anything the government can do about this?" he asked. "This is a disgrace."

"Mr. Brennan, the police would like to see these children disappear," Father Davila replied. "And they are doing their best to make that happen."

Just then Mango returned and appeared agitated and upset.

"Raymondo tells me that a few of the boys were out scavenging early this morning, and some did not return. He thinks Manuel was one of them."

The priest's face darkened and he called to Raymondo.

"I want you to take these men to the place where Manuel and the others were begging." Suddenly, the boy began to cry and shake, repeating a sentence in Spanish over and over.

"Raymondo thinks that the authorities caught Manuel and took him somewhere. He keeps mentioning the torture house."

"Let's get going," Mango commanded, and they turned to follow Raymondo back along the dark corridor and up the stairs. When Mango lifted the heavy sewer cover, moist night air filled Paul's nostrils and he breathed it in quickly, wanting to cleanse his lungs of the putrid air below. Paul followed closely behind Raymondo, and in the glow of the street lamps he could see his thick, matted hair full of crusty scabs and red patches. Mango stopped the boy after a while and thrust a twenty dollar bill into his hand.

"To be sure we get what we're after," he said as he turned and winked at Paul.

Raymondo kept running ahead peering around corners to be sure there were no police around. Finally he took them behind some abandoned buildings and walked down into a ditch, pointing to an old wooden shack. He began to shake again, and Mango threw his arms around the boy.

"Wait here, Raymondo, while we go down to the little house."

Paul and Mango crept along the weed-choked, well-worn path and drew their guns. Mango quickly walked around the outside of the little shed. Finding no one, they both climbed the two steps leading to the door. The latch was broken and the bottom hinge was falling off. Mango pushed the flimsy door open with his foot and they went in. Paul's heart jumped as his eye caught three nude children lying in a corner, their hands still tied behind their backs. As he got closer he realized they were all dead, seeing their eyes staring up pitifully at the ceiling. Mango turned one over and they saw fresh cuts and burn marks on the child's back.

"They've been tortured," Mango murmured, and picked up an electrical cord from the opposite corner of the room. "The blood stains are relatively fresh," he stated.

"Can you tell if one of them is Manuel?" Paul asked nervously.

"Hell, no! I have no idea what he looks like. Guess we'll have to call Raymondo down to identity these kids."

Paul wandered over to the oldest looking one and gazed down into his lifeless face, immediately recognizing the resemblance to the boy's sister.

"That won't be necessary, Mango. This one reminds me of Gaby. They both have the same high cheekbones." Paul wiped a tear away and untied Manuel's hands.

"We still need to identify the others. Go get the kid" Mango ordered.

"You can't think of making him come in here! He was shaking just telling the priest about this place."

"The priest will want to know, Brennan. And besides, these kids see death all the time. They're used to it, believe me. It's a part of everyday life for them, like watching cartoons was for you."

"Mango, you have no heart."

"Listen to me. The police did this and Carlos may have already been told about it. It gives you the perfect opportunity to get the film while Carlos is occupied with this mess. Manuel was his brother-in-law. He'll want a full investigation. So go tell the kid to get down here and then get over to Carlos's place right away. I expect to see you at the hotel, preferably before morning."

Paul closed the door and walked up to Raymondo, not knowing how to tell him. Somehow he knew from Paul's eyes, and he ran down to the house. Seething with rage, Paul began running, trying to put the hate behind him. All he could see before him were Manuel's frightened eyes and Gabriella's tear-stained face as she heard the news. He caught the first taxi he found and sank into the dark recesses of the back seat to hide his pain.

CHAPTER 18

"I am sorry, but Mr. Rojas and his brother are not here now, Señor Brennan" the maid stammered. "I don't know when…"

"I only want to get a few things I left here," Paul interrupted. "I'll just be a minute."

"No, you better come back tomorrow when the master is here," she firmly replied, and began to close the door. "I am not supposed to let anyone in when they are not here."

"But you know who I am," Paul protested. Just then he heard a voice calling out in Spanish. The maid answered with his name.

"Let Mr. Brennan come in, Antonetta," Carina commanded. The maid opened the door reluctantly and Carlos's sister came toward him dressed in a tight, black lace outfit barely covering her thighs. She held out her hand to him.

"Where have you been?" she asked seductively, while she shot a menacing glance at the maid, who quickly disappeared up the stairs.

"I just came back to pick up a few things I forgot. Are you on your way out tonight?"

"Not now. Let's have a drink in the study," she suggested, removing her black silk shawl and hanging it on the hall tree.

"I'd like to get some things from my room. You start mixing." With that he sprinted up the stairs before she could object. He found his room and twisted the knob, but it wouldn't budge. Pushing his leg into it, he tried to force it open. It was locked tight. Giving up, he went down to the study.

"Do you know how to make a martini?" he asked her as she held up a bottle of Scotch and studied its label.

"Of course I do. But I thought you drank plain Scotch. Here."

She handed him a drink, then turned around to make one for herself.

Lowering her voice, she added "Antonetta doesn't approve of my drinking, but as you can see, I get my way in this house."

"I'll bet that's not the only thing Antonetta doesn't approve of," Paul commented, while he settled back on the leather couch and wondered how to get the film.

"She hates me. She doesn't like the way I dress and says I am disrespectful. She expects me to stay at the hospital and sit at my father's bedside with my mother."

"How is your father?"

"Oh, he's all right. He may be coming home tomorrow. I miss him. He's the only one in the family who really understands me."

Carina sat down very close to Paul and stretched her arm behind his head across the back of the couch. She looked intently into his eyes.

"How long will you be staying, Paul? I can call you Paul, can't I?"

"I'm leaving tonight, actually. That's why I need to get my things. Carina, why is my room locked?"

"Antonetta keeps the doors locked when guests are not here. But I can get the key for you if you like."

Paul took the drink out of her hand and pushed her long hair away from her ear. Moving closer to her, he whispered "Yes, I would like that very much." Just to make sure she understood, he kissed her lightly on the cheek. Then she began to laugh, an impish grin spreading over her youthful face.

"If you want the key you must come to my room to get it!" Then she jumped up and ran out calling for the maid.

Hoping that Carlos wouldn't come home just yet, Paul began to climb slowly up the stairs and waited impatiently on the landing, turning toward the front door to see if there were any signs outside the windows of approaching cars. Suddenly Carina came up behind him and covered his eyes.

"That bitch didn't want to give it to me!"

"Where is it?" he demanded.

She removed her hands and kissed his earlobe. "You must come to my room first." Carina began to run and Paul chased her down the hall, following her into her room and closing the door.

"The games are over, Carina. Give me the key."

"Find it on me!" she taunted, and he grabbed her and threw her on the bed. Thrusting his hand between her breasts, he felt for the cold metal object. It wasn't there. She smiled and spread her legs apart. He slid his hand down along her leg and pushed her lace skirt up to reveal bikini underwear.

"Take me," she whispered, clutching his neck. He rolled her over and his fingers groped for the key. Finding it on the bed he scooped it up and roughly pushed her aside.

She raised her head with an angry look, pulling her skirt down.

"You spoiled little tease!" he shouted, as he jumped off the bed and ran out of the room.

"Wait until my brother hears about this!" she yelled back.

Jogging down to his room, he shoved the key into the lock and opened the door. Swinging the heavy armoire door open, he reached down and lifted the loose bottom board. There in the corner, the little roll of film sat obediently, waiting for his return. Dropping it into his pocket, he swiftly unplugged his fax and grabbed his small suitcase.

I'm out of here, he thought as he closed the door. Just as he started down the stairs, the front door opened and Carlos stepped into the foyer!

■■

Carlos's gaze travelled upward and their eyes locked for an instant.

"PB. You're back!"

"Not for long. I'm just picking up some of my things."

"How are you? And how did you get away?"

"How the hell do you *think* I am, Carlos? I was beaten and robbed and then kidnapped."

"You have to believe me, Paul. I did everything I could to free you from those murderers. They were just immovable."

"Oh, come on, Carlos. You and I both know you traded me for your father."

"What good son wouldn't? In the end I had no choice. You are all right, so forget it. Come and have a drink before you leave."

Paul put the suitcase and fax down near the door and followed him into the library.

"What will it be, Brennan? Scotch?"

"I've already had a drink and I sure as hell don't care to drink with you."

Carlos looked at the two empty glasses on the table near the sofa and walked over to pick one up. Holding it up to the light he noticed red lipstick stains on the edge. "So you have. It looks like my sister has been the perfect hostess tonight."

"We just had one drink to say good-bye."

"That's what you say!" pointing a rude finger at him. "I wonder what Carina would tell me."

"Get off the macho routine, Carlos. You know she whores around and doesn't give a damn about what the family thinks. I didn't touch her."

"My sister may be forward but she's not a whore!" Carlos's eyes blazed and his neck muscles tensed. He started toward Paul, then stopped and went back to the bar to mix a drink.

"What do you want from me, Brennan? You were an errand boy, that's all. I told you up front that my main concern was getting my father back."

"How is he?"

"Better. I'm bringing him home tomorrow. I'm sure he would love to see his savior." He turned and raised his glass to toast Paul.

"Sorry. I have to get back to my job as a reporter."

"Oh yes, your paper. Do they know you are also working for your government?"

"After tonight, I no longer work for any government. Good-bye Carlos. When you see Gabriella, tell her I said vaya con Dios. Treat her well. She's the best of your possessions."

"That's right, Brennan. She's *my* possession. I'm warning you to stay away from her!" Carlos's back arched and he swung clumsily around, throwing his drink against the wall.

"Stay away from my wife!" he screamed as he lunged toward Paul, who braced himself and deflected Carlos's punch away from his jaw. Paul shot his clenched fist into Carlos's angry face, causing him to reel and fall. Paul turned and walked to the front door and let himself out.

CHAPTER 19

The fresh night air filled his lungs as Paul strode briskly down the path and out the gate. He turned right and continued to the end of the street where he had told the taxi to wait. Climbing in, he pushed a twenty dollar bill into the driver's outstretched hand and told him to go downtown to the hotel.

He sped along the wide avenues past huge houses surrounded by iron gates. Winding driveways led up to magnificent facades, and he wondered what kind of secrets those walls hid. The road began to descend and the city lights below came into view. They were soon downtown, weaving through traffic and stopping abruptly at lights. While they waited, a bus pulled up and discharged some passengers. Paul's eye caught a tall, dark-haired woman among the group. She sprinted ahead of the others and hurried up one of the side streets. His heart skipped a beat. He was sure it was Gaby! The cab jerked into motion and drove away as he turned his head to try to follow her. She was gone. What was she doing here now? Why would she have come? Did Carlos know she was in town? Had he been with her? These questions continued to swirl in his mind as he tipped the driver and walked into the hotel lobby and up to the desk.

The clerk recognized him. "Good evening, Mr. Brennan. Mr. Cenera has reserved a room for you. Four eighteen."

"Thanks. Have someone take my bags up. I'm going to my friend's room."

"But Mr. Cenera is not in right now."

"Oh. In that case, I'll take a look at my room."

The bellhop swung the door open majestically and Paul stepped into a luxurious suite not unlike the one Mango had in Cuba. The rooms were bathed in shades of muted yellow, and the half-open drapes revealed a splendid view of the city. As his feet sunk into the plush carpet, he turned to reward the boy and close the door. Beyond the sitting room was a well-stocked bar and he walked over to pour himself a Scotch. Spotting the bedroom through heavy damask curtains pulled back with thick tasseled ropes, he entered and ran his hand across the silk bedspread which dressed the huge circular bed.

In the center, a small box wrapped in silver foil slept peacefully, its white ribbon attached to a small beige card. Paul grasped the end of the ribbon and pulled the gift toward him. Small black letters said "Nice reward for a job well-done, PB. See you soon. M"

Paul opened the lid and pulled out a new wristwatch pager, its luminous numbers glowing in the semi-darkness. Getting up, he noticed a mini-fax with attached phone in one corner, and a computer system set up on a small white table in the opposite one.

All of a sudden the phone rang. Paul walked over to the nightstand to pick it up, wondering where Mango was tonight.

"Is this you, Brennan?"

"Yes, Paul Brennan. Who is this?"

"Finally found you! Been trying for days. It's Brian Matthews from headquarters. Hold on until I switch to a private line."

"I'm glad you called, Brian. Have you spoken to Mango tonight?"

"No, not since this morning."

"Well, I've decided I want out. I'm sure he plans to speak with you soon. I've had enough."

"You can't do that, Paul. I need you. Now more than ever."

"Sorry, Brian. Tonight I completed my last assignment. Get yourself another agent."

"You've got to stay on just a bit longer, now that we've discovered the possibility of a mole in our operations."

"Mole? What exactly does that mean?"

"Someone or some group is providing assistance to the drug cartels."

"No kidding. We already know that Cuba is involved."

"No, I don't mean that. There's an inside connection."

"Inside the department?"

"We don't know how far it goes. We'd like you to stay on until it unravels a bit more. You could be instrumental in leading us to some clues. I trust you, Brennan."

"Look, I took the photos you wanted and nearly got myself killed!"

"Do you still have the film?"

"Yes, but as soon as I turn it over to Mango I'm released from all commitment, according to him."

"Listen to me. Don't give that film to anyone. Put it into locker number twenty-five at the airport. I'll have it picked up."

"But Mango is expecting me to give it to him. What'll I say?"

"Tell him I told you to release it to me. I'll deal with him. I'm still your superior until I get the film. Then you can stop working for us and return to the US. But I'd feel a whole lot better if you stayed."

Brian's voice sounded honest and Paul could sense a worried desperation, almost bordering on fear. He had always trusted this man.

"All right. I'll hang on to the film until I can deposit it. But I'm not staying here more than a few days to arrange a flight back to New York. I'll do what I can until then. But I want out. It's too dangerous here. "

"Call me tomorrow, Paul. And be careful."

Paul hung up and rolled the film around in his hand, hidden deep in his jacket pocket. Who should he believe? Was State just being paranoid as usual? Or was there really someone in Washington undermining the work in South America? And what about Gaby? Feeling torn and guilty for wanting out, he dialed Mango's room and got no answer. Grabbing the room key, he headed for the elevator and took a taxi to the airport.

CHAPTER 20

"I'm only staying for the funeral, Carlos. Then I go back to my father." Gabriella swept her long hair up on the top of her head and pinned it in place. Carlos stood behind her in their bedroom and caressed her long pale neck. As he began to kiss her ear, she abruptly pulled away.

"You must be distraught from all the news about your brother, my dear. I'll get you a drink."

"I don't want a drink!" she screamed. "Can't you see I don't want to make love to you now? Don't you care about Manuel at all?"

"Of course I care. Why do you think I called you as soon as I was told about it? My jet got you here faster than any airline."

"Ever since I joined your family, my father and I have only known terror and sadness. Now, two of my brothers are gone. I couldn't even tell my father about Manuel. It might have killed him."

"I tried to persuade your brother to stop hanging around those hoodlums. He refused my help."

Gabriella's eyes burned with rage. "What kind of help did you offer, Carlos? A job dealing drugs? You drove him to a life of stealing and deception, whether you want to admit it or not."

"Don't blame me for the sins of your family, Gabriella," he yelled back. "Your father begged mine to accept you and marry you, and I have always tried to help all of the Santiagos!"

"Help? You had Roberto killed and stole my father's ranch. Now my uncle is even taking orders from you. Must you control everyone?"

Carlos clenched his jaw and moved toward her, twisting her arm behind her while he cupped her chin with his other hand.

"No. You are the only one I need to control. Start acting like the wife of Carlos Rojas." He let go of her arm and held her in a strong embrace, pushing her against the wall. Struggling to get free of his grip, she softened for a moment and kissed him sensuously. Then she noticed the bruise on his face and moved back.

"What happened to your face?"

"Oh, your concern is touching, my dear...just a little fight with your lover." Carlos rubbed his cheek and winced.

Gabriella gasped and put her hand up to the bluish red mark. Pushing her hand away, he grabbed her neck and pulled her head toward his and almost whispered into her ear.

"Stay away from him. He could be dangerous for us. He works for his government as well as being a reporter."

"Did you hurt him?" she shrieked.

Carlos lowered his tone of voice. "A good wife shouldn't care."

"What do you expect me to do, wait around until you get tired of your playmates? I know you have other women, Carlos. Is that what a good husband is supposed to do?"

"I am going downstairs for a drink. Leave the door unlocked," Carlos instructed, as he turned and left the room.

Gaby rubbed her neck and walked to the mirror to see if his grip had left any marks. She stared at her face and began to cry. Then she thought about Paolo. Was he all right? What had Carlos done to him? She felt overwhelming sadness for her brother and for herself. What a terribly sad life she had led so far, and yet, when she thought about Paolo, she couldn't help but be a little less sad. He was a good person who would help her. Maybe he was the only person who could lead her out of this dark time and into a less hostile world. She stared into the mirror and crossed herself, saying a silent prayer to her savior.

■■■

Street noises conspired with the insistent beat of the rain against the windowpane to wake him, and Paul pushed the digital clock around to reveal the time. Tossing the sheets over his head, he turned away and tried to fall back to sleep. All he could think of was finding Gaby. Perhaps she wasn't the one he'd seen last night. Maybe he just *wanted* it to be her. Deciding to go back to Puerto Rico to see her, he threw off the covers and padded into the bathroom to wash his face.

Someone knocked at the door. "Room service," he heard a young voice call out.

"I didn't order room service. You've got the wrong room!"

A strong fist suddenly began pounding. "Open up, Brennan! I ordered it for you."

Paul opened the door when he heard Mango's voice, and a maid pushed a gleaming silver cart into the sitting area, with Mango following close behind.

"We've got lots to talk about, Brennan. I got in so late last night I didn't bother to come and see you."

"Out on the town, Mango? I thought you didn't go in for night life? Or was it a private affair?" Paul asked sarcastically, as he sat down and uncovered a steaming tray of scrambled eggs and sausage.

"Actually, it was sort of a private meeting, but not the kind you're thinking of, Brennan. Mango pulled a chair up to the table and started pouring coffee into Paul's cup.

"Still trying to keep me here, Mango? By the way, the new pager was a nice bribe and this room is wonderful, but I'm sorry that I won't get to enjoy it much longer."

"I promised you a proper setup when we were in Cuba. And after you hear what I've got to say, I'm certain that you'll change your mind about going." Mango bit into warm bread and poured some coffee.

"Look, I told you last night, I've had enough. I've also spoken to Brian Matthews about getting out of all this."

Mango's face lost its confident glow. "What did you call him for?" he growled.

"I didn't. He called me last night. I told him I'd only be here long enough to make arrangements to fly back."

"Didn't he tell you to wait until the DEA found a replacement?"

"No. It was obvious that he'd prefer me to stay on, but he understands." Paul sipped his coffee and tasted the eggs.

"Well, you may not want to go now. Your girlfriend is in town."

"Gaby? I thought I saw her on the street last night. What's she doing here?"

"It's only natural that a sister would want to attend her brother's funeral."

In all the confusion he had totally forgotten about Manuel. Of course that was why she came to Bogotá!

"Where is the funeral, Mango? I want to be with her."

"I don't think you should go there. You'll see her soon enough."

"You don't understand, Mango. She probably needs me right now."

Mango put down his cup and slammed the silver lid down to cover the eggs.

"No, *you* don't understand. Listen to me. She wants to help us. She's ready to be part of our operation, but on one condition. She insists on working with you."

"Gaby wants to help us? I don't believe it. Why?"

"She is torn up about losing two brothers. She doesn't like what Carlos is doing to her family. Frankly, I think she is ready to leave him."

"Did *she* approach you about this?"

"After the police removed the body, I went back to tell the priest. Apparently the authorities had informed Carlos right after the murder and he had his wife flown in. She had to go to the morgue so she could identify the body and make funeral arrangements. She told

Father Davila she wanted to speak to me, so he sent her to a church downtown and told me to meet her there last night."

"Where is she staying?"

"Last night she stayed with Carlos, but I told her I'd get her a room here so you two could work together. She'll be checking in around four p.m."

"So that is why she wasn't with Carlos when I was at their house earlier. She was meeting with you. But why would you tell her that I'd work with her before asking me?"

"I figured you would want to be with her. I didn't know you were going to bail out on me. Where is the film I told you to get?"

"I don't have it. Brian instructed me to leave it to be picked up by someone from headquarters. He said he'd explain everything."

Mango's expression again turned sour and he quickly jumped up, banging his fist on the table. "What time did you drop it?" he yelled.

"Around midnight, I guess. I'm sure it's been picked up by now."

Mango went over to the phone and dialed some numbers. After a few seconds he repeated some codes that Paul didn't understand. Then he hung up.

"Why are you so upset, Mango? The film is on its way."

"That's just it. Matthews constantly denies me promotions and I wanted to control this job and prove to him I am worthy of more respect."

"I'm sorry, but I had to take orders from him. He's my superior."

"Our deal says you're committed until *I* get the film! So are you staying, Brennan?"

"I have to talk to Gaby about all of this. Reluctantly, I'll stay until I hear her explanation."

"Good. Meet us downstairs for dinner at five p.m. That'll give her time to settle in. I've got to run."

Finishing the last piece of sausage, Paul pushed his chair away and grabbed the phone book, flipping through the Ds until he found Davila.

■■

By noon a humid soaking rain had descended over Bogotá, and dark clouds blocked the pale sunlight. Father Davila and Paul followed the lone hearse by car as it left the church on its way to the cemetery. Through the car window Paul could see some of the children he had met in the sewers coming out of the cathedral. One girl carried a white lily and leaned on Raymondo, the boy who had led them to the shack. Pregnant Maria followed them, still counting her chain of rosary beads.

"All these kids have left is religion," Father Davila intoned. "Their parents and family have forsaken them, and the government doesn't care."

"At least they still have something to believe in," Paul added.

"Someone, you mean" corrected the priest. "They believe in God but have very little faith in the future. Hope is something they find hard to grasp."

"Can you blame them Father?"

"No, I guess I can't."

They drove on, winding their way out of the center of the city, climbing a bit higher. As they neared a bend in the road, the hearse dipped down and out of sight, turning onto a narrow lane that led to a grove of trees.

"Carlos might not want to see me. Perhaps I should stay in the car. I don't want to cause Gabriella any trouble with him."

"Why wouldn't he want to see you, Mr. Brennan?"

"I have a confession to make to you Father. I hit him last night, in self defense of course!"

Father Davila smiled kindly and said, "You should have turned the other cheek. But I will grant you forgiveness if you join the family today and help us bid farewell to Manuel. Besides, Gabriella might need your support today."

They parked the car and got out. They could see Carlos and Eduardo struggling to lift the casket out of the hearse. Tomás and his uncle José helped, and the four of them began walking up to the gravesite. Carlos's father walked along beside Gaby, his wife, and daughter to the burial plot. Carlos shot a menacing glance at Paul but said nothing to him, as he and Father Davila arrived. Paul backed away and stood apart from the rest of the group when the priest began to read scripture. Gaby didn't look up. The huge brim of her black straw hat hid her eyes, which Paul guessed were red and swollen. Her black-gloved hands trembled slightly as she gripped the white prayer book, and her high heels sank deeper into the mud as she shifted her weight. The rain had stopped, but a fine mist clung to everything, making the air heavy with grief. Wishing she would look at him, he fixed his gaze on her, blocking everything else out, and repeated her name silently over and over. Slowly the curved brim of her black straw hat tipped upward and she looked out from underneath. At first her glance was unfocused and distracted. Then she recognized him and a faint, wistful half-smile broke through the despair. Their eyes locked and Paul knew she had been comforted a little. Father Davila finished and handed Gaby a shovel. She dropped a bit of dirt onto the coffin, and after kissing a white rose she was carrying, threw it on top of the mound. Handing the shovel to Carlos, she walked over to Paul and grasped his arm. He whispered to her under her hat that they would talk soon. Then he withdrew and walked quickly back to the car to wait for the priest.

"Mr. Brennan!" the elder Rojas called out, and Paul turned to see him hurrying over.

"I wanted to thank you for helping to free me. I never had the chance before."

"That's all right. Your son really did more to release you than I did. How are you?"

"I'll never quite recover from that horrible affair, but with my family's care, I will get better. Will you be returning to your country soon?"

"Yes, quite soon, Mr. Rojas. I doubt if we will ever meet again."

They shook hands, and the old man turned to rejoin his family. Raindrops suddenly began to pelt Paul's face and he rushed to the car.

"Poor little Manuel," he thought as he gazed up at the grey heavens. Then he wondered if perhaps he wasn't one of the luckier ones, tucked under an angel's arms, protected from all the sorrow and heartache he had known on earth.

CHAPTER 21

Paul and Mango sat at the bar and drank their mojitos while they waited for Gaby.

"Women always keep you waiting, Brennan. Order another one."

"No, thanks. I'll nurse this one until she gets here."

Mango leaned over closer to Paul and said, "I spoke to Brian just after lunch. It seems like the department is unusually concerned about leaks. He wants me to call in every day to report."

"Oh, I thought you already knew about this so-called mole."

"I had heard rumors, but you know how Washington can be sometimes. I don't believe everything I hear."

"I don't either. Listen, Mango. Leaks don't really interest me right now. The only thing I'm concerned about is getting disentangled from this situation as soon as possible, and of course making sure Gaby is safe."

"Don't you think they are mutually exclusive, Paul? You might have to stay in longer to guarantee her safety."

Just then the elevator door opened and Gabriella emerged, dressed in the same black crepe dress she had worn at the funeral but without the hat and bolero jacket. Her hair was swept up and twisted to the side, held with two tortoise shell combs. She spotted them and waved.

As she got closer, Paul could see that the diamond earrings and heavy perfume couldn't hide her sadness. She looked drained and downcast.

"Good evening gentlemen." Her shallow voice lacked its usual color, and Paul's nod couldn't coax that tenuous smile he had learned to expect.

"Paolo," she half whispered, taking his arm. He pulled her close to him as Mango paid the bill and they walked over to the table.

"You'll be okay. I'm here now," Paul whispered to her as they sat down next to each other.

"Drink, Mrs. Rojas?" Mango asked.

"A pisco, thank you."

As Mango studied the menu, Paul slipped his hand into hers under the table and he could feel her beginning to relax a bit. The waiter promptly took the drink order and they settled back in their chairs.

"Thank you for being there today for me, Paolo. It meant a lot to me."

"I wanted to be there for you. Did you know Mango and I were the ones who found Manuel?"

"Yes, Antonio told me. And please, Tonio, call me Gabriella."

"All right," Mango answered. He winked at her. "The beef is excellent tonight. I recommend it."

"I don't think I can eat much tonight. I have no appetite."

"Order something anyway. The waiter will be hurt if you don't and you might find that you are hungry once the food arrives. You need to be strong in the next few weeks." Mango again looked at her intently, trying to send her a message.

Paul's voice interrupted their conversation. "Here comes the waiter with her drink. Let's order so we can get down to business. I am anxious to know what Gaby has on her mind."

Gaby took the pisco, while Mango and Paul ordered huge plates of beef.

"Bring us a third plate in case the lady changes her mind," Paul told the waiter. "And bring us a bottle of a good red wine."

"Tell Paul what you told me last night, Gabriella. If he agrees, I'll fill you both in on my plans for your first assignment."

Gabriella sat up straight and strained to focus her tired eyes on Paul.

"When I married into the Rojas family I thought I was buying stability for myself and my family. I was wrong. The advantages I receive as the wife of Carlos Rojas are not worth the losses I have had to endure. I feel certain that he will end up destroying me and my family. I want to save what is left. I must."

"You say you bought your way into the marriage, Gaby?" Paul interrupted.

"Yes, that's what I call it. The Rojas dynasty looks at every relationship as a business venture. Carlos uses people for his own ends. I am convinced that he doesn't really love me. His numerous affairs are proof of it."

"Go on," Mango insisted.

"I feel that I have failed my family with this marriage. I want to help bring Carlos to justice and avenge my brothers' deaths. My father would never forgive me if I didn't do what was right. Carlos is slowly killing him and I have to stop him."

She lowered her voice as the waiter brought wine glasses and opened the bottle, filling all three with a warm burgundy.

"I don't know everything about Carlos's work, but I know a great deal. I'm sure Carlos doesn't suspect how much I am aware of things. I am a good listener. And Eduardo is a great talker." She laughed a little, perhaps from the drink or from nervous exhaustion. Then she grew more serious.

"I know I can help your government, and I am willing to cooperate. But only on one condition." She turned and looked at Paul.

"Paolo must work with me. He's the only one I feel I can trust. And your government must secure my safety. I must admit I am frightened. I know what Carlos is capable of doing."

"If Paul agrees, I think I can assure you the best protection possible. Our government is very anxious to stop the flow of drugs to the US and to put men like Carlos out of business."

Paul cleared his throat and looked at Mango. "I think we need to hear some specific information before we agree to bring you in on this, Gaby. Don't you agree, Mango?"

"Of course. I can see Paul's point, Mrs. Rojas. We're risking our necks for you and your family. We need some assurance that you will cooperate fully to help us capture your husband."

Gaby shot a hurtful look at Paul.

"Don't you think I really want my freedom from Carlos? Do you think I am playing some kind of game with both of you? It took a lot of courage to even come here to meet you. I'd be giving the US the information they want in exchange for my freedom. Isn't that enough?"

Paul took her hand and looked into her eyes.

"I'm sorry if you misunderstood me, Gaby. I want what is best for you and your family. I also want to be convinced that it's worth putting my life in danger. I've already been beaten and kidnapped. What more can you tell us that would let us know you are being sincere about this offer?"

"Carlos works with all of the cartels, making it easy for them to ship the drugs out from ports he controls. He uses boats with fake bottoms and launders money in other countries. He recently negotiated some arms deal with Cuba. I know his travel patterns, his contacts, and the banks he uses. Several European countries are providing military training to the drug organizations. Who do you think is paying them?"

"All right, you've made your point. Her information sounds right, Brennan. Are you in or out?"

Paul started to speak when he saw the waiter bringing two large plates of steaming beef, and an empty plate which he put in front of Gabriella.

"This looks great! Don't you want some of mine, Gaby?" Paul asked

"No. Just bring me another drink," she said to the waiter.

"First I'd like to corroborate some of her information with the DEA if we can. Then I'd need to hear your plans for the assignment before I commit to it," Paul announced.

"You can call Brian tonight after dinner" Mango replied, digging his fork into slabs of meat. "The details of the initial assignment are not that involved. My hunch is that her uncle José is instrumental in shipping drugs out to other countries, so that they can then be sent up to the US. I need to know where, how, and when so we can trap him. I'm sorry, Gabriella, but it's the only way to get to Carlos."

"But my uncle is innocent! He does what Carlos tells him to do."

"Accessories have to pay the price. If you're worried about your uncle, forget helping us, Gaby. Do you want to get Carlos or not?" On hearing her balk, Mango turned on the pressure while he cut his slice of beef, dabbing a piece into some steak sauce and chasing it down his throat with some red wine.

"What's the rest of your plan, Mango?" Paul interjected.

"We gather all the information we can get on Carlos, including names, addresses, agenda plans, and bank records. If we succeed in trapping Gaby's uncle, we can use him as bait to catch Carlos. It could take a few weeks, though. Your assignment will be to go to Lima and follow the money. Find out exactly what José's role is and what he does for Carlos. While you're both working on that angle, I'll continue to tail Carlos."

"And what happens to Gaby after this is all over?"

"That's up to her. If she wants to be free from the Rojases we can arrange to get her to the US, where she can ask for asylum and file for divorce."

"Where does Carlos think you are right now, Gaby?" Paul asked.

"I told him I was only staying for the funeral because I had to return to my father. Carlos thinks the priest wants me to talk to the children tomorrow, and I also told him I need to have the death certificate notarized and to meet with our lawyer to make changes to my will."

"There isn't much time, Brennan. You've got to decide soon so I can get you both out of here and on to Lima and the assignment, before Carlos gets suspicious. She can call him in a few days and tell him she's in Puerto Rico."

"No, that won't work," Gaby protested. "He always insists that I travel on his private jet. I don't want to do anything out of character."

"She's right Mango. Think of something else...something to keep Carlos busy here for a few days."

"Let's finish dinner so that you can call Matthews and make up your mind, Brennan. In the meantime, I want to go over some details with Gaby and figure out a better alibi for her."

Paul put a few slices of meat on Gaby's plate when her drink arrived, and they lingered a bit over coffee. Then Paul got up and left them to return to his room and call Brian Matthews.

"Brian? It's Brennan calling from Bogotá. I need to get some info corroborated."

"Talk to headquarters about that. Are you staying on?"

"I'm not sure yet. That's why I need some answers from the DEA before I decide. Did you get the film?"

"Yes, it's quite interesting. I think the mole has lifted its head a bit. But we still need you down there. I want you to continue taking orders from Mango, understanding that I will override some of the decisions from time to time. And promise to call me daily. Things are going to heat up pretty fast down there."

"Mango was pretty upset about not getting the film. Did you explain things to him when you spoke to him this afternoon?"

"No I didn't. You tell him to control his Latin temper and remind him to call in every day. He has to remember he's not running the show down there...I *am!*"

"I may have a new partner soon, Brian. I'll let Mango fill you in."

"You tell him I want to know all about this new partner. Be careful, Paul. Remember, trust no one."

Paul hung up and called headquarters to forward his questions. He hoped the answers would come back soon. Then he dialed the front desk to get Gaby's room number. He had to talk to her alone.

CHAPTER 22

Paul sipped the cognac that had just been delivered to his room and wondered if Gaby had come upstairs yet to hers, three doors down. He wondered how long Mango would keep questioning her. He peered out into the empty, silent hallway. No sign of her. He kept his door open just a bit and waited. Soon he heard the elevator bell, and he saw Mango and Gaby emerge. Stopping before her door, Mango took the key from her hand and unlocked her door. Then he placed his hands on her shoulders and slid them halfway down her arms before planting kisses on both cheeks. Paul burned with jealousy. How could he be so forward? They had only just met briefly the night before! As she turned away to enter her room, his hand glided down her back and patted her behind. As soon as the elevator door closed, Paul locked his door and sprinted down the hall to her room.

Rapping lightly, he whispered "It's Paolo," through the crack in the door. He heard a click and the clatter of the chain, and she suddenly appeared, her long hair falling across her face.

"May I come in?"

Throwing her arms around him, she pulled him closer and shoved the door closed with her foot.

"Paolo, I need you," she sighed as she began unbuttoning his shirt.

"Wait, Gaby. I want to talk to you first." Leading her to a chair, he sat her down and pushed the hair out of her eyes.

"Are you sure you know what you are doing, leaving Carlos and trying to turn him in? Aren't you afraid of the consequences?"

"It's something I must do, Paolo, even if I have to risk my life." Her voice seemed faraway and sad, but nonetheless determined.

"Carlos has many influential friends. If he's caught, he may find ways to free himself. We both know he'd be angry enough to punish anyone who caused him trouble, even his wife. I'm afraid for you, Gaby."

"Don't be afraid, Paolo. Work with me so that I can be free of him. He is destroying my family."

"He could destroy both of us. Do you want that?"

"I know you were put in danger and I wish I could have prevented that, my darling. I prayed every night for you."

Trying to change the subject, Paul walked to the bar and poured a Scotch for her.

"Here, drink this. Maybe it will dull your pain."

Cupping the glass with both hands, she sipped it. Paul tried to lighten his tone.

"I watched you and Mango outside your door. Is he moving in on me already?"

She looked up into his eyes and the little smile slowly began to appear.

"You just don't understand Latin men, darling. He was only being friendly. He didn't mean anything."

"What about his parting shot…that little love pat?"

"Just a Peruvian custom, my dear," and she put the drink down and lifted her dress up over her head, revealing a black strapless bra and silky half slip. "Let's not waste precious time talking about him."

Paul scooped her up and carried her to the bed. Her nimble fingers deftly removed his shirt and caressed his chest, and he hastily unhooked her bra.

"Your arms are so strong, Paolo," she sighed, as he pulled her closer underneath him and their lips traded intimate secrets. She brushed hers across his shoulder and he whispered "I love you," into her ear, while she nestled close, trying to shut out all her sorrow.

"I dreamed about you after I left you," he told her. "We rode horses along the beach."

"I wish I had dreamed that dream too, my darling."

He pulled off her slip and underwear, and gently pressed his body against hers. She melted into his, as if wanting to drown in physical release so that she could forget her sorrow and her fear for just a moment. He folded her into his arms, wanting to shield her from her grief but knowing he couldn't. He could almost feel her sadness as they both began to breathe harder, and he placed his hands around her head, putting his mouth next to her ear and repeating "shh" as if to calm a frightened child. As their rhythms flowed together she finally softened, letting go of the pain for just a minute. She had lost so much, so fast. Paul wanted to give her back some of the happiness she deserved, but wasn't sure he knew how. They fell into a blissful sleep, holding on to each other, not sure of anything except the tender affection they had both found.

CHAPTER 23

Gaby stirred a bit and turned over, falling back into a semi-slumber. Seeing her eyelids begin to quiver, Paul watched her drift peacefully into a little dream, wondering if he was in it. As he pushed a strand of glossy dark hair away from her face, her eyes fluttered open, and her little smile reappeared, lighting his world with joy.

"Good morning, Mrs. Rojas," he whispered as he slipped his arm around her neck. "Did you sleep well?"

"Better than I have in a long time." She leaned over and kissed his cheek. "Do me a favor. Don't call me Mrs. Rojas anymore. I don't like to be reminded of my husband. Besides, Mango will probably invent new names for us while we are working together and we must get used to them."

"Sorry, darling. You're right." He reached for a cigarette while she propped herself up on several fluffy pillows.

"I must admit that when I saw his bruised face, I didn't really care about his pain. I was more concerned about you."

"That's because you love me, my dear Gaby." He leaned onto his elbow and playfully rubbed noses with her.

"Do you love me enough to get involved in this job, Paolo? Mango wants an answer this morning."

Before Paul could answer the phone rang. Gaby picked up the receiver and handed it to Paul.

"I'm having breakfast for two sent up there, Brennan. Then you had better give me a definite answer. Did you hear from State yet?"

"No, not yet, Mango. I'll see you in an hour."

"If you decide to work with us, be in my room by eleven. I've worked out all the details."

Paul hung up and pulled Gaby's hair back and off her neck, planting a kiss on her creamy shoulder.

"Breakfast is coming. Then I'll talk to the State Department. Don't worry."

She looked at Paul as if he were her last hope. Then she got up and disappeared into the bathroom.

■■

The maid pushed her cart along the hallway, throwing Paul a sly glance as he left Gaby's room. He opened the door to his room and pushed the drapes aside, noticing several glossy rolled sheets on the fax tray. He grabbed them and began to read. It was the State Department's opinion that Gaby's information sounded credible and was most convincing. They urged him not to quit.

Sounds like Brian got to them, he thought as he began tossing some things into his bag. Somehow Gaby's security remained uppermost in his mind. He couldn't let her down now, no matter how much he wanted to stop working for the DEA.

At eleven sharp he took the elevator down to Mango's suite and knocked.

"Come in Brennan," a male voice yelled, and he turned the knob. Gaby was seated on the swivel chair in the sitting area, looking over some papers, while Mango tapped out messages on his computer.

"Well, what's the word, Brennan?" Mango shouted over his shoulder.

"I'm in. State believes her information."

Gaby's eyes had been riveted on his, and as soon as she heard those words, her little hint of a smile grew wider and her eyes became alive with hope. She got up and came toward him, dressed in a bright green, tight-fitting dress.

151

"Paolo, I'm so grateful. I will never forget this."

Seeing her matching green bowler hat on the table, he asked

"Shouldn't you still be dressed in mourning colors, Gaby?"

"Not anymore," answered Mango. "She's Mrs. Brennan now and you two are visiting her aunt in Lima before you both return to New York. Gaby will put on a black dress when she goes to visit Mrs. Santiago and Tomás. Otherwise, it's life as usual for a young married couple."

Aren't you afraid Carlos will find out what she's doing?"

"It's all taken care of, Brennan. This morning Carlos will find out that his jet has engine trouble and can't fly. Gaby will call him from the airport and tell him she will stop to see her aunt and then fly to Puerto Rico from Lima on a commercial airline."

"Engine trouble? You work fast, Mango!"

"Not me. Our government. Now here are your tickets. Send me a message at least once a day. Gaby has the list of warehouses you need to visit and a few contact names. Try and trace a shipment, and gather as much documentation as possible. And above all, be careful. Any questions?"

"How far do you want us to go with this, Mango?" Paul asked.

"Don't leave South America, but you can go into other countries if you need to. My main objective is to confirm my suspicions about her uncle, and to get enough evidence to trap Carlos. Follow any leads. Try bank accounts. Gaby plans to take you to her father's ranch. I'm sure something is going on there."

"His ranch? Won't Carlos be watching that place for us? That sounds too dangerous for her."

"Carlos won't be anywhere near the ranch. The assembly meets this week and he will need to be in the capital near his father to protect him. Besides, his girlfriend's thirtieth birthday is in two days, and he's planning a big surprise party for her."

Gaby looked sad and went back to the sitting area. Paul walked away from her.

"Did you have to mention that, Mango? You know she is still upset about her brother's death."

"She stopped caring for Carlos long ago, Brennan. Now don't forget to destroy that list once you both memorize it. If you get separated, return to Bogotá. Your rooms will be waiting."

The two men shook hands. Mango embraced Gaby and then turned to grab the bags. Paul took Gaby's hand and they walked to the elevator. Wishing they were off to enjoy a honeymoon instead of a dangerous assignment, he tried not to let his apprehension show. But Gaby knew how he felt. She leaned over close to his ear.

"Vaya con Dios, my dear," she whispered, and he looked into two deep black pools of sparkling courage.

CHAPTER 24

Brian Matthews pressed the accelerator to the floor and sped along the highway, wondering who it was who wanted to meet him so urgently downtown, and why it had to be secret. He had called his wife and told her he wouldn't be able to join her for dinner, and had cancelled a late-day appointment. Just "drinks at a sky-top penthouse," the messenger had stated…a matter of vital importance concerning our efforts to curtail the drug trade to the US.

Matthews parked the car in the underground garage and took the elevator up to the top floor. He rang the bell and a maid finally answered and showed him to the balcony where he was served a drink and told to wait.

As he gazed out over the bustling rush hour traffic below, he heard footsteps. He turned to see a tall, balding stranger come toward him and offer him his hand. They made polite small talk for a few minutes. Street noises drowned their conversation, and the maid came out to see if they needed anything before she left.

Brian was thinking about Paul Brennan, hoping to receive a phone call from him that evening, a phone call that might lead him to some firm answers. He was perplexed about this person who was not making much sense, talking about the ineffectual drug enforcement laws and the turmoil caused by them. The stranger suddenly threw wads of thousand dollar bills onto the small round table between them and beckoned for Brian to take them.

"In return for what? My silence? My inefficiency? My ineptitude at stopping leaks?" Brian stood up and kicked the table over. The bills flew up and a breeze caught some of them and carried them up and over the balcony railing and down into the streets.

When the maid arrived the next morning, Brian's car was still parked where he had left it in the underground garage.

****

Sliding his arm across the cool soft sheets, Paul reached out for Gaby. Feeling nothing but empty space he opened his eyes and then realized she was not beside him. Mango had thought it would look better if she spent the night at her aunt's house without him. She would return to the hotel at noon where they would have lunch before working on assignments.

He held his arm up and tapped out a message to Mango on his new pager. "Arrived Lima…will start work this afternoon…missing my bride already…. PB."

Grabbing the phone, he ordered room service. Eating alone had never bothered him before. Suddenly he felt strangely alone and sad without Gaby, and he tried to think of things to do until lunchtime— a dip in the hotel pool, perhaps? Then he suddenly remembered Brian. He had sounded so worried the last time they had spoken. He dialed his number in Washington. His secretary answered.

"This is Paul Brennan. I'd like to speak to Brian Matthews."

"I'm sorry, Mr. Brennan. Mr. Matthews has not yet arrived."

"When do you expect him?"

"We're not sure. He should have been here by now. Would you like to leave a message?"

"No, I'll call back in a few hours. Thank you."

Thinking that it was strange that Brian wasn't in the office, he threw on a robe and opened the drapes. Menacing grey clouds hung down over the city, making its poverty all the more depressing. He grabbed a magazine he had bought at the airport and leafed through it while he waited for breakfast to arrive. "If only I had a copy of this morning's paper," he half said aloud to himself. Suddenly he began to think about his colleagues at the news office and how much he missed working with them. He hadn't spoken with them in days. Why not call? He picked up the phone.

"Hello, Dave? It's Paul. I'm in Lima. How are things?"

"We're about ready to meet to decide tomorrow's lead story, so I can't talk long. What are you doing in Lima?"

"My work here has been extended. Didn't State get in touch with you about it?"

"We haven't heard from them since we cleared you to go to Cuba."

"That's strange. I was sure Brian would have told you I had gone to Bogotá. It sure seems like a long time since St. Thomas."

"We gave you a week, PB, and it's been a bit longer. You owe us one hell of an article."

"Don't worry. You'll get a bigger article than you ever dreamed. But I'm not sure when. Things are somewhat uncertain down here."

"By the way, who did you say was to contact us?"

"Brian Matthews. He's working with the DEA. I just called Washington and they told me he hadn't arrived at his office yet."

"Hold it. His name was mentioned in the early morning news flashes. I'm scanning the files. Here it is under DC…looks like he won't ever be contacting us."

"Why? What happened?"

"He fell from an eighteenth-story balcony downtown last night. The FBI is investigating."

"Oh my God! A suicide?"

"No one knows. The apartment is owned by an entrepreneur who has property in Aruba and had worked for an oil company."

"What's his name?"

"Not given. FBI asked the press to withhold. All it says is that the maid found him when she arrived for work. She said a tall man and Matthews were drinking on the balcony when she left at six p.m."

"Have they questioned the apartment owner?"

"It's very sketchy. Says nothing about him, so I assume he hasn't been found yet. I'll let you know if anything more breaks on this, Paul. Your fax still on?"

"Of course it's on. You know he was so worried the last time I spoke with him. He was onto something."

"I've got to go, PB. Great hearing from you. Get your tail back to the Big Apple so we can catch up with a few beers at O'Neal's."

"I'm not sure I'm coming back, Dave. I'll be in touch."

CHAPTER 25

Paul watched from the bar as Gaby strode swiftly through the lobby and stopped in front of the gold elevator door. She pressed the up button and leaned back on her heels, gazing intently at the floor. A single strand of pearls broke the monotony of her black dress. She carefully removed her straw hat and pulled at her hairpins. Shaking her head slightly from left to right so that her twisted locks would come loose, she seemed as if she wanted to free herself from something.

"Want another, sir?" the bartender asked.

"No, my table should be ready any minute."

Paul had left a note on the bed for Gaby to meet him in the restaurant. He couldn't stop thinking about Brian, and tried to search for clues in their last conversation but nothing seemed to make sense. Why hadn't he told him more? Was he to take his orders from Mango now, or would someone take Brian's place? All he could do was proceed with his plan until someone contacted him.

"Hello, darling." Gaby slid her arms around his neck and kissed his cheek. She had changed into a light pink suit, and a rose-colored scarf held her glossy hair out of those sparkling black eyes.

"Oh, I have missed you, Mrs. Brennan. Our table is ready." Paul signaled for the waiter and they sat down in a discreet corner. Gaby opened her menu.

"I finally got some answers from Auntie after we had coffee this morning. And last night I found some bank statements in Uncle's desk drawer. I have an appointment with the bank officer at three p.m."

"So, my little wife has been working hard, I see." Paul took her hand in his and looked at her, trying to find an answer to all this mystery.

"Paolo, you looked worried. Has anything happened?"

Paul had decided not to tell her about Brian. He didn't know why. He just wanted to wait, to see what developed.

"No, I just feel so helpless. We've been in Lima for almost a day and you're the only one who has done any work."

The waiter took their lunch order and collected their menus.

"Don't worry. You'll get your chance. Here's my plan. While I'm at the bank, you can scout the wharves and see what's going on. Auntie tells me Uncle spends a lot of time with a man named Caballa. He works on pier 12."

"I thought you and I would be working together on this, Gaby. You know my Spanish is almost nonexistent."

"I had a better idea. Tomás will meet you and help you find information. It would look strange for a couple to be wandering through warehouses. But no one will suspect Tomás. He will be at Cesar's café at two o'clock."

The waiter brought their drinks and placed a basket of warm bread between them.

"'Have you spoken to Mango this morning, Paolo?"

"No, but I called New York and talked to a colleague. He's looking into something for me. Gaby, aren't you afraid of what might happen if Carlos finds out we're working together? Because I certainly am."

"Is that what is worrying you, my darling?" She put her bread knife down and shot him a commanding look.

"Please don't even think of him. He is too busy with his father, his business, and his other women to bother about us. But we must move quickly. We shouldn't stay in one place too long. Have you memorized all the names and places that Mango gave us?"

"That's all I did yesterday besides swimming and eating. You know, Gaby, I really missed you last night." He took her hand again and kissed it.

"I missed you too. But we must be strong when we are apart. We cannot always be together."

The waiter brought over two warm plates, and filled them with salad and beef slices.

"I found a marvelous little salsa club we can visit tonight, Gaby. I've always wondered how it feels to dance with you."

As she picked up her fork and lifted some food to her lips, she replied, "Haven't we danced together already, in our dreams?"

"Maybe in your dreams, Gaby. Not in mine."

"All right. If I'm not too tired after dinner we can go. But only if you bring back some important information. Let's meet upstairs around seven. You know how late dinner starts here. It will give me a chance to rest a bit and contact Mango with my news."

Suddenly it seemed to Paul as if she was running the show. No more helpless wife on the run from her tough husband. Paul felt displaced. Or maybe he just imagined that she was more assertive now. Perhaps she had always been that way and he had never noticed until now.

CHAPTER 26

The streets were deserted at siesta time. Even the bus had stopped running. The sun had finally burned through the dense foggy mist, and the air felt fresher and cool. Paul read a newspaper while he sat at a tiny round table at the sidewalk café, waiting for Tomás. The bar was empty, except for two old, weathered sailors playing checkers under the laboring ceiling fan in a back corner. As he swigged his warm beer, he wondered what Caballa looked like. He wondered if he would lead them to the truth. Just then he spotted the boy turning the corner.

"Hello, Tomás. Sit down. Would you like a Coke?"

His eyes lit up and Paul flagged a waiter.

"You know I am working with your sister. Do you think you can help us?"

"I will do anything for my sister, Mr. Brennan."

"Good. What we need to do is to find Mr. Caballa. Do you remember his first name?"

"I met him once. I don't remember his name, but if I see him I'll know him."

"Do you come down here often with your uncle?"

"Last year I did when I visited him. He showed me some odd-looking boats."

"Do you know where pier 12 is?"

Tomás sipped his Coke and looked toward the docks. He pointed to a huge red building next to some rusting hulks.

"That's it. Over there."

"We must be careful, Tomás. We will begin by walking along and watching. If you see the man, point him out to me. Then go and speak to him. Try to find out when they will be sailing and on which boat. Pretend you want to go with them. But don't say anything about me. Can you do that?"

"I will do my best for my sister. But what if I can't find him?"

"Talk to some of the other sailors. Ask them when they will take their next trip, and where they will go. I'll be close by. Then you tell me what you found, okay?"

"Okay. Can I have another Coke, please?"

"Sure you can. And when you bring me the information, this is yours." He held up a crisp ten dollar bill.

■■■

Gabriella looked around in the ornate bank lobby, and suddenly recognized an old girlfriend behind one of the teller's cages. She glanced at her watch. Two forty-five. It would not be polite to arrive at her appointment at three, since the custom was to arrive a few minutes late. Gaby walked up to the teller's cage.

"Hola! Maria. Remember me?"

"Hola! Gabriella! How are you? It has been so long since we have talked!"

"I am fine. I need to get some information for my uncle who is sick. Can you tell me his bank balance and give me a list of the last three months of transactions?"

"It is not allowed for anyone but the account holder to access that information." Then in a low voice she told her "but for you, I will do it. It will take some time, though."

"That's all right. I have to speak to Mr. Montero at three. I'll pick it up after I see him."

"How is Carlos?"

"He is about the same. He travels a lot for his business. We do not see each other often."

"Are you happy, Gabriella?"

Gaby looked wistfully at her old friend. "I'm not sure anymore what happiness really means."

Maria looked at her quizzically. She raised her voice as her supervisor walked behind her. "Give me the account number, please."

Seeing an impatient gentleman standing behind her friend, Maria whispered "I have other customers, Gaby."

Gaby quickly pushed a copy of a bank statement toward her friend. They said good-bye and Gaby took the elevator to the top floor. She lingered outside the office and read notices on the wall. Two men quickly brushed past her and ran down the stairs. At 3:10 p.m. she announced herself to the receptionist and was ushered into the plush interior of the bank president's headquarters.

■■

Paul shuffled along the quay, looking like a lost tourist holding a map and his guidebook, wondering how Tomás was doing. He had disappeared into one of the warehouses twenty minutes ago. Paul wandered up and down the piers and watched the fishermen quietly mending their nets, or eating empanadas and drinking cold beer. Deciding to look for him, he walked over to the building that Gaby's brother had entered, and peered over a rusted metal window frame through dirty glass panes.

All he could see were huge wooden crates scattered throughout the warehouse, along with piles of torn fishing nets and broken traps. In one corner, rusted hooks and cables were haphazardly laced through heavy anchors, while next to them lay neat coils of rope and piles of heavy sailcloth. He saw no movement. Then he spotted a small corner office near the front of the building. He moved toward the other side of the building and looked in through the grimy cobwebbed window. Several file cabinets stood near the door next to a desk piled high with papers.

Paul decided to enter the building since there didn't seem to be anyone around. If Tomás had no luck, perhaps he could find a sailing schedule or some other evidence. Heaving the heavy door open, he quickly reached the office. He tugged at the top drawer of the cabinet and it came open. It was stuffed full of stamped documents. The second drawer was locked. He glanced at the papers on the desk. Flipping the top folder open, he noticed a name at the top corner. The files seemed to be in last name order. Searching for Caballa or Santiago, he sifted through the files until he saw "Rojas" and abruptly stopped.

Pulling out his miniature camera, he began snapping shots of pages, while trying to listen for sounds and occasionally glancing at the window to spot anyone who might look in. As he turned the fourth sheet, he heard voices at the other end of the warehouse. He quickly closed the file and dumped the others silently on top. Turning to go, he looked up to see a blackboard he had not noticed when he had entered the room. Names, destinations, ship names, dates, and cargo were neatly listed. The third one down jumped out at him. "Caballa, Suriname, Mirabelle, 10th." No cargo listed. The other six all listed types of shipment. The voices grew louder and he hurried out of the office toward the front door, hoping he wouldn't be noticed. Then he recognized Tomás's voice among the deeper male speakers. They were still closer to the other end of the warehouse, so he let himself out and walked around to the back and then away from the building.

He and the boy had planned to meet each other at the café, so he crossed the street and took a seat to wait for him. It wasn't long before he saw Tomás waving. He ordered a Coke and a beer from the waiter, and watched him run toward the café.

"Well, young man, what did you find out?"

"Señor Caballa is not here today but he will come in two days. The sailors promised me a ride on the airplane."

"Airplane? Are you sure?"

"Yes, one said they fly to Leticia every week to take supplies there."

"Did they say what kind of supplies or what happened to them?"

"I don't know exactly. No."

"When are they leaving?"

"Tomorrow morning at ten if the fog lifts by then."

"Will Caballa go with them?"

"He meets them in Leticia, I think. Did I find out what you wanted, Mr. Brennan?"

"You did fine, Tomás. Here is your reward." He stuffed the bill into his hand.

"Here comes your Coke, too." The thirsty boy gulped it down and Paul swigged his beer.

"Tomás, if you think of anything else you forgot to tell me, you must let your sister know about it right away. I'll tell her to call you tonight to chat."

"Okay. Mr. Brennan, do you have any brothers?"

"No, I never had any. Only a sister."

"I only have a sister now too. My brothers have all gone to heaven and my father is on his way, my aunt says."

Paul looked into this twelve-year-old face and wished he could wipe away his pain, but he knew he couldn't. At least he had his sister and his aunt and uncle. Lots of kids had less.

"How about if I order you another Coke before I leave?"

"That would be great!"

"Don't worry, my little friend. Gabriella will take good care of you. And I am sure you will see your father very soon."

Paul walked over to the waiter to order the second Coke and pay the bill. Then he said good-bye and walked to the stop to wait for the next bus to go back into town.

CHAPTER 27

The crowded bus heaved and lurched its way through the city streets, reminding him of the Fifth Avenue local at rush hour in New York. Humid, stifling air blew in through the windows and mingled with the sweat of the passengers. Heavyset housewives with varicose veined, unshaven legs tried to balance packages between their knees while keeping their swollen calloused feet firmly on the floor, to shift their weight when the vehicle turned a corner. Old men and young boys stood two rows deep, the men puffing foul-smelling cigars and the boys trading jokes and eyeing the young females, who wore low-cut blouses and tight skirts.

As soon as the bus grinded to a bumpy halt one block from the hotel, Paul jumped off, glad to be set free. The hotel lobby felt cool and comforting, and he decided to visit the bar before going up to change and wait for Gaby to get back from the bank.

Sipping his drink, he started to think about Brian again. What had he stumbled on in Washington? Maybe Mango would have a clue. In any case he had to move fast since a plane was leaving tomorrow and Caballa would arrive the next day. Draining his glass and throwing some money onto the marble counter, he caught the elevator. When he entered the room, the fax was busy shooting out pages. He grabbed the cover sheet. It was from Dave at the paper. Brian's death had made front page news in the evening edition.

He began to study the faxed article. Dave had underlined some sections. The owner of the penthouse, Richard Melas, said he had lent his apartment to a friend that night to conduct some business dealings. The friend had taken a flight later that evening, but Melas wasn't sure of the destination and hadn't seen his friend that night. The suspect's name was still being withheld pending investigation. Strange, he thought. Melas was obviously covering up for him. Where the hell had Melas been? If you lend a friend the apartment you ought to know how long he plans to use it.

Brian's body had marks about the neck and there had definitely been a struggle. Autopsy results would take a few more days. The FBI was checking airport manifests on flights out of DC that night. Dave promised to send him more tomorrow.

Throwing the report on the bed, he took a quick shower and slid into a terrycloth robe and lit a cigarette. Paul took a deep breath and closed his eyes. Brian's words about the mole raising its head rang in his ears. Entrepreneur who worked for an oil company in Aruba…what was the connection with Carlos's operation? He suddenly remembered that he had more pressing concerns, namely, how to get to Leticia and find out about the plane. He began to tap out code to Mango, then stopped, thinking that he should wait to include Gaby's information from the bank. He glanced at his watch. Almost six p.m. She would be here by seven.

Paul pulled on his swim trunks and took the elevator to the indoor pool. It was deserted. Perhaps a swim would help him think things through. The regularity of the laps began to clear his brain and he swam evenly back and forth, picking up speed after the second trip across. Something Dave had said on the phone came back to him. The words "Haven't heard anything since you were cleared for Cuba," stung him. He was astonished that Brian hadn't told them he had left Cuba for Puerto Rico and then had flown to Bogotá. He had assumed communications were clear and that Paul's whereabouts were being reported to his paper. Perhaps Brian had told someone else to do it? Or maybe he was never told? Paul thought everything had to go through Brian's office. How could he not know where Paul was at all times? Had Brian wanted to keep Paul's movements a secret from the press? Why? His heart began to race and he slowed down.

Stepping out of the water he vigorously rubbed his legs with a towel and dried his back. He decided to call the research department and order more information on Melas…what he looked like, where he travelled, how much he was worth.

He shaved and dressed, his mouth watering for a good steak and a bottle of red wine. Picking up the phone, he dialed the little club to book a table for two for ten p.m. He couldn't wait to get Gaby into his arms. Maybe she was the one he had been waiting for all his life. He closed his eyes and began to imagine them together on a dance floor, samba rhythms pounding in their ears…as he drifted off into a little cat nap, her face came toward his, the hint of a smile growing ever larger.

He woke with a start and glanced at his watch. It was 7:50 p.m. Where was she? He checked the bathroom to see if she had come in and was showering; finding no one, he splashed water on his face. It was dark outside and the lights were turned on downtown. He closed the drapes. Grabbing the phone, he dialed the desk downstairs.

"No, she is not in the bar, Mr. Brennan."

Slamming the phone down, he began to get angry and pace. Why couldn't women be on time? She said seven sharp. He turned on the TV and tried to understand the words. Changing channels, he finally found a news program. Pictures of rubble downtown filled the screen and he watched in horror as they carried bodies out on stretchers. Then the news anchor repeated Banco de Crédito and he gripped the remote and strained to hear more, but she had moved on to a different story.

Paul dialed the desk again and asked what had happened.

"A bomb went off in the lobby at closing time. Many were injured, sir."

"What hospital would they have been taken to?" he shouted.

"Wait. I will find out and call you a taxi."

Paul hung up and grabbed his jacket, tearing out of the room and down the hall.

CHAPTER 28

The hospital corridors were eerily silent, as the echo of Paul's footsteps followed his frantic gait down long, narrow hallways, which suddenly twisted and changed direction. Since the elevators on the ground floor were out of order, he clamored his way up a straight iron staircase, his shoes ringing out hollow metallic noises each time he took a step. Pushing the swinging door open, he came out into a reception area and went up to the desk.

"The nurse downstairs told me to wait here to see…"

The nurse behind the desk looked up and gave him a blank stare.

"*No hablo inglese*, señor." She turned back to her paperwork.

"Well who the hell *does* speak English around here?" he yelled.

A female doctor heard him and rushed over.

"Sir, you must lower your voice! There are injured people here."

"I need your help. Can you tell me if Mrs. Rojas was brought in recently? She may have been a victim in the bank bombing. Please."

"I'll see what I can find out. Sit down over there and be quiet."

The doctor quickly disappeared, and instead of sitting on the plastic bench she had pointed to, he wandered down the hall, peeking into examination rooms trying to find Gaby. At the end of the corridor, a coffee machine stood against the wall, and he dropped some coins in and bought a cup. While he sipped it, he slowly strolled back to the reception area and leaned against a pillar, watching two young nurses struggle to push a patient toward the OR. Two women tearfully followed alongside whispering some prayers. Probably his mother and wife, Paul thought. He began to fidget and looked at the clock above the reception desk. Nine p.m. If the explosion had gone off around four o'clock, and Gaby had been hurt, she must have been here for close to four hours. Suddenly someone touched his arm, and the female doctor motioned for him to follow her.

She took him into a small conference room. A grey haired elderly doctor in a long white coat pointed to a chair, and Paul thankfully sank down into it.

"This is Dr. Morrera. He examined someone he thinks is Mrs. Rojas when she was brought in."

"My name is Paul Brennan. How is she Doctor?"

"Good evening, Señor Brennan. You are American, I think?"

"Yes."

"I spent a year studying at Johns Hopkins. Grew terribly fond of Big Macs! I wish I had a quarter of Hopkins's resources to build this hospital into what it should be, Señor Brennan."

"Look, I'm only a poor journalist, but if you take good care of Gabriella I'll write articles to support your cause. Now how is she?"

"I have to admit I'm a bit confused. You called her Mrs. Rojas, didn't you? The ID card in her purse said Gabriella Brennan. Is she your sister?"

"We are related, yes."

"Oh, I see. Do not worry. She will be fine…only a mild concussion and one broken rib…some cuts and bruises of course. She apparently had just gone out the front door on the ground floor when it happened. She was quite lucky. Some of the tellers were killed. However, she did lose the baby."

"Baby? I didn't know…can I see her now?"

"Her husband is with her. She was given an injection for the pain and will receive a sedative soon. I suppose it wouldn't hurt for you to see her for a few minutes."

"How long must she stay here?"

"At least overnight and perhaps a day or two more. If she doesn't feel dizzy or weak in the morning, I might allow her to go home. She's in room 231."

"Thank you, Dr. Morrera. I won't forget your kindness."

Paul walked out into the hall after shaking the doctor's hand. The female doctor pointed to the one working elevator. "First door on the right." Paul pushed the button and waited. Then he remembered. The doctor told him Gaby's husband was with her! How did Carlos find out and get there so fast? How could they continue working together? Now how could she become free of him?

As he neared the room he heard voices. Peering in, he saw the edge of her bed and heard her speaking in Spanish to someone. The man leaning over her was certainly not Carlos. Then he recognized Mango's short husky frame and distinctive voice.

Paul hastened over to Mango, who turned when he heard footsteps near.

"Well, Brennan. It's about time." Paul walked to the other side of the bed and took her hand. Leaning down he kissed her tenderly and squeezed her hand again, not taking his eyes off her. "How are you, darling?"

Before she could answer, Mango blurted out an explanation.

"Gabriella phoned me from the bank to call in some information right before the blast. When I heard about the bombing on the radio, I drove straight to the scene. I told you I wouldn't be far away."

Paul put a smile on his face and looked sideways at Mango.

"Rather clever to pass yourself off as her husband." Winking at Gaby he added, "I thought **I** was supposed to be playing that role."

Gaby gave him a weak smile, and Paul bent down again and kissed her bruised cheek.

"It was easier to get to see her that way," replied Mango. "Now I'll let you two visit for a bit. I want to talk to you later, Brennan. Meet me downstairs in the lobby in a few minutes." He pressed Gabriella's hand and left the room.

"So, how are you really feeling? Tell me the truth."

"I am very tired and sore. I am so glad to finally see you."

"What happened at the bank?"

"First, I asked an old friend who works there to get me copies of some of my uncle's bank statements. Then I went upstairs and met the bank president. He was polite but refused my requests for any information on Carlos's accounts. He insisted on being able to inform Carlos, so I declined. I think he is a good friend of Carlos's father. I was just going out the front door when the bomb went off. I don't remember anything else until I woke up at the hospital in the emergency room."

"Thank God you are only bruised. The doctor said you may be able to go home if you have a good night. Are you still dizzy?"

"No, but I am very thirsty. Could you hold the water glass so I could reach the straw? They taped my side and it hurts when I move or breath."

Paul reached for the glass and held it out to her. Then she leaned back against the pillows.

"What did you and my brother find out at the warehouse?"

"I was able to walk around unnoticed in the warehouse, and found a file with "Rojas" on the tab, so I shot a few photos of documents. I also noticed a blackboard with sailing dates and ship names with cargo. I think I know what ship Caballa is using and the date of sailing."

"That's great! Did Tomás speak to anyone?"

"Yes. He spoke to some of the sailors. Caballa wasn't around, but they told him they plan to fly out tomorrow to Leticia at ten with some kind of shipment. They offered to take him along. Do you think we could let him go to find out how and where they send the cargo? It might be helpful if you talked to his aunt so he can go. He's awfully excited, and it might get us the information we need."

"Give me the phone, Paolo. I'll call my aunt. I can do some more snooping while I recuperate there. I'll tell my brother he'll get his plane ride." She cleared her throat and sat up.

"Do me one more favor, darling. My friend at the bank printed me a list of my uncle's bank account activity for the last year. I put it in my purse. See if you can get it from the hospital clerk. They must have taken it from me when I arrived. Perhaps you can study them."

As she reached for the phone, Paul propped her up on the pillow and took her bruised face in his hands and kissed her.

"I love you, Mrs. Brennan" he whispered.

As he watched her dial and speak to Tomás, he thought how lucky she was to be alive, and how fortunate he was to still have her around. She put the receiver down.

"My aunt will pick me up whenever I am released. My brother will be at the warehouse at 9 a.m. to meet the sailors. He knows the way, and I don't think you should be seen with him again. Maybe you could meet him somewhere else once he returns."

A stern voice behind him reminded them that visiting hours were over, so he bent down once more to kiss Gaby good-bye. Just then, a thought ran through his brain. Why had she called Mango with the information? Why hadn't she waited to tell him? He searched her tired eyes and decided to ask her.

"One more thing, darling. Why did you feel you had to call Mango with the bank news? Why didn't you wait to tell me so we could give him my message with yours?"

Her calm expression suddenly became disturbed and a bit fearful.

"I don't know. I just thought you would be out and I should contact someone as soon as possible."

"Gaby, let's promise each other from now on to confide in each other first, before Mango or anyone in Washington, okay? I spoke with the newspaper office this morning. They think Brian Matthews was thrown off a balcony and killed. My stateside contact will be changed, and I'm not sure how this affects Mango's position."

She raised herself and leaned into him, grabbing his jacket lapels.

"Are they letting him go?" she demanded.

"I don't know what is happening in Washington, Gaby. Things are confused right now. Just try to get better so we can get back to work."

She settled back on her bed and closed her eyes. Paul kissed her forehead and turned, walking out of the room and down the hall. Stopping at the second floor reception, he asked about Gaby's purse, writing her name and room number on a piece of paper. After a few minutes, an elderly man shuffled out of a back room with her purse under his arm, his stooped shoulders making his wrinkled neck disappear underneath his heavy, bulging face muscles. His bony fingers pushed the purse across the dusty desk, and Paul quickly took it and opened the clasp. All he could see was her handkerchief and wallet. In the bottom a lipstick case and a pen rolled around among some loose change. The list was gone!

CHAPTER 29

What had happened to it he wondered? He stared down at the purse, then up at the old man. He thrust his hand deep down into the folds of the silk lining, hoping to find it in a corner. No luck. As he withdrew his hand, the wallet tumbled halfway out and he noticed that the flap was unsnapped. Perhaps she had folded the list and had put it inside with the bills, or tucked it away in a pocket next to her checkbook. He carefully opened each side but found nothing but bank slips and a few faded business cards. Then the picture section fell out and he tried to scoop the cascading plastic file back together. There on the top was a small wedding photo of Gaby and Carlos. Across from it was someone else he barely recognized. It was a snapshot of a young Antonio Cenera, before he took on the code name Mango, proud and defiant. Scrawled across the bottom was a faded fountain pen-inked inscription in Spanish. So they *had* known each other long ago! Mango looked all of sixteen, although he may have been older.

Paul had seen enough. Pushing the contents back into the purse, he slid it back over the counter and motioned for the old man to take it. He was sitting on a chair about to doze off and slowly pulled himself up and lumbered over to the counter, a snarl on his face because he had been disturbed.

Pushing the elevator button, Paul leaned against the wall to wait and lit a cigarette. He had never been sure of Gaby's feelings for him, and now this. He decided to act as normal as possible to Mango, who by now must certainly be aware of Brian's death.

The elevator door opened and Paul got out. Mango stood a few feet away with his back to Paul while he read a wall poster.

"Anything interesting?" Paul asked, as he came up behind him.

"Warning about AIDS," he replied as he turned to face Paul.

"What did you want to talk to me about, Mango? I'm pretty beat and I haven't had dinner yet."

"In that case, let's grab a bite and talk at the restaurant. There's a little spot I know a few blocks from here."

"How do you know Lima so well, Mango? I can't imagine that you would have spent much time in this neighborhood near the hospital."

"I was born in this hospital, Brennan. Didn't you know I grew up on the outskirts of the city?"

"No, I thought you were Cuban." They walked out the front door and down the street.

"I am. Well, half Cuban. My father left Peru to work on a construction site in Cuba. That's where he met my mother."

As they walked along, Paul began to piece some ideas together. Gaby had lived with her aunt in Lima while she was in high school. Perhaps they had lived in the same area or had the same friends. He didn't want to ask too many questions. He wondered if they had dated and he felt a small pang of jealousy. Perhaps Mango had known her when she was more tender and innocent. Maybe he was her first lover. Now Paul understood why they had seemed so friendly that night in the hallway, as he'd watched from his hotel room.

"Here it is, PB. They have great steaks imported from Argentina and terrific local seafood."

"I've had my mind set on a steak since this afternoon. But I imagined that my dinner companion was better looking."

They took a back table in a secluded corner and since there were no menus, Mango called the waiter over and ordered two prime cuts, one rare and one medium. As the waiter placed wine glasses in front of them, Mango leaned toward Paul and declared, "I've got some news from Washington."

"What sort of news?"

"Changes. I've been told to take over for Brian for a while until someone else can do his job. Looks like you're taking orders directly from me now, Brennan."

"'Did Brian get a promotion or did he offend someone?'"

Mango's eyes shot Paul a penetrating glance as he sipped his wine that had just been poured. "Didn't you hear what happened? I thought you knew. Brian was found dead several days ago."

"Dead? What happened?"

"No one knows. It looks like it might be a suicide."

"I doubt that. I never would expect it of a man like Brian who seemed happy enough."

"Well, you just never know these days now, do you?" Mango replied. "Perhaps the tension was too much for him. The DEA was pressuring him to make more arrests. He just wasn't accomplishing enough down here."

"The last time I spoke with him he was somewhat concerned about a possible leak. He told me he thought the mole had raised its head a bit, as he put it."

Mango's face hardened and he blinked a few times, turning his head down and away. Their steaks arrived and Paul proceeded to stab into the savory herbed flesh, chewing the juicy morsels and downing them with the woody tasting red wine.

"So, is that all you wanted to talk to me about, Mango?"

"No. Just this…since Brian is no longer the boss, I have to fly to Washington for a week or so. You'll have to continue here on your own. You and Gaby can check out bank leads and see what you can find out at Carlos's ranch until I return. Just call in to me every day."

"Gaby said she had picked up a list of her uncle's bank account statements. Do you have it?"

"Oh, yes. She told me to look at it and see if I could make sense of it. I'll be glad to make you a copy back at the hotel."

"So you say you grew up around here? How old were you when you left?"

"Eighteen. I was one of the lucky ones. I made some contacts with the right people and got free of this place. I moved to Cuba and settled there."

"You never mention a wife. Were you ever married?"

"Once. A long time ago. It just didn't work out. It's hard to keep a wife when you're in this business. I guess I'm a little like Carlos Rojas. My job is more important than my personal life. Just look at Gaby. Do you think he makes her happy?"

"I don't know. You'd have to ask her. But I doubt it. Didn't Gaby live in Lima when she was young?"

"Lima is a big city. Gaby and I are from two different worlds."

"But you didn't live in two different worlds back then, did you?"

"Gaby was just a teenager when she lived with her aunt here. Then she left when her mother died. But she didn't live like I did."

The waiter came to see if they needed anything and left the check. Paul didn't pursue the questioning, and they finished their wine in silence. Mango finally broke the lull.

"It's getting late. I've got a plane to catch in the morning. Let's go to the hotel so I can make you a copy of this."

As Mango left the table to call a taxi, Paul wondered what he had been like as a youth in Lima, and what his real connection was to Gabriella Santiago Rojas.

CHAPTER 30

Paul tossed his head back, downed another double Scotch, and then signed the hotel bar bill. He staggered to the elevator and got in, pushing the button for his floor. Confusion swirled through his brain as he thrust his hand into his jacket pocket and felt for his key. Falling onto the bed, he kicked off his loafers and hugged the pillow. The liquor had not helped him to sort out the mysteries. He'd have to wait until morning. Hearing the distant whir of the fax, but too tired to get up and read the message, he quickly drifted away, his head pounding and ringing with names, faces, and questions.

■■

The harsh daylight assaulted his swollen eyelids as he gently raised them to admit a bit of cloudy glare bursting in from the open drapes he had forgotten to close. He needed aspirin, or coffee, or both. Grasping for the phone, he dialed room service and ordered a light breakfast.

Pellets of hot water stabbed his back as he showered; he let the steam fill his lungs and the spray sting his neck and face. Slowly he came alive and began to think more clearly. Pieces began to fit, and he wondered why he hadn't seen the signs earlier.

As he toweled off, he conjured up scenes from the past that now started to make a little sense. There were still many missing parts and lots of answers yet to be revealed, but he was getting closer. Anxious to read the fax transmission, he threw on a robe and grabbed the sheet.

"Richard Melas, born Miami, 1956...half Cuban, half American. Dark eyes, 5 foot 10 inches. Medium build. Father is a respected businessman. He left Florida in 1978 to work for oil refinery in Texas. Suspected of ties to drug dealers. Arrested once but charges dropped. Frequent visits to Aruba. He's being held in DC. Prime suspect in Matthews murder. Research."

Suddenly two quick jingling rings assaulted his ears and he grabbed the phone.

"Brennan speaking."

"Paul, its Dave from the *Times*. I've got some updates for you on Brian Matthews's murder."

"Go ahead. I just finished reading Research's fax on Melas."

"The FBI is pretty sure Melas didn't do it. They've tracked his friend, the guy he lent his apartment to that night. He took a 9 p.m. flight to Havana that evening. His name is Alberto Ruiz."

"What's he look like?"

"Very tall, balding. He's quite a social butterfly. Likes to party and dance and spend nights with prostitutes. Apparently he's got close connections to the cartel. The CIA is investigating, but State thinks he's a glorified hit man for them."

"Do me a favor. Tell Research to find out all they can on Antonio Cenera, otherwise known as Mango. He works for State. I think I'm on to something."

"I'll have them get on it right away. You should hear from them before tonight. Be careful."

Paul began to dress, ideas mixing in his mind like chocolate sauce in a marble cake batter. Was Ruiz the tall bald guy on the dance floor in St. Thomas and in Havana? Had he made the phone calls to Paul's room? How did Mango get Gaby's letter back so easily at the Cuban beach? Why was it stolen?

A knock on the door announced his breakfast and the steward wheeled the cart in, shoving the bill under Paul's nose. He signed it and shut the door. Tearing a warm roll in half and smothering it with butter, he chewed the bread and breathed in the fresh, strong aroma of coffee that he poured into his cup. Why had Mango been so incensed when he gave the film he had taken at Carlos's house to State for a pickup? How could he have missed all these clues? Had his feelings for Gaby clouded his perception? He decided to take Brian's advice from now on and trust no one.

He had no time for leisurely conjecture anymore. He had to have a car, in case he had to leave in a hurry. Opening the morning paper, which lay next to the soft-boiled egg cup, he noticed headlines at the top and pictures of the bank bombing on the front page. He scanned the list of names in the text of those killed or injured, but Gaby's name did not appear. His head was beginning to feel better, and he decided to head downtown to see about renting a car.

■■■

The private airplane revved its jets as one of the sailors pushed Tomás up over the little step into the back seat.

"Buckle up now," the sailor yelled over the droning engine, and the boy obeyed. The pilot turned his head and looked at the boy.

"What's *he* doing here?" the pilot shouted.

"It's okay. This is Carlos's brother-in-law. I promised him one ride. His sister said it was all right."

The pilot turned back to the cockpit dials and checked gauges, snarling a bit. Soon the plane took off and climbed up over the mountains, losing itself in the deep blue sky above the lush green below.

■■

The phone was ringing repeatedly as Paul forced the key into the lock and hurried to open the door. Reaching across the bed, he seized the receiver and swung it to his ear.

"Brennan," he said, half out of breath.

"Paolo? It's Gaby. I'm at my aunt's house."

The sound of her voice no longer thrilled him the way it used to, and he answered her in a cool, professional tone.

"How do you feel?"

"I'm much better. The doctor wants me to rest for several days, though. Then I'll join you at the hotel."

"Take as long as you like, Gabriella. You need to recover before you start working for us again."

"Paolo, you sound strange. Is anything wrong?"

"No, Mango and I just had a few too many drinks last night, that's all. I've been busy checking out the bank statements you were given. Looks like your uncle's in pretty deep. Did you find out anything else?"

"Not yet. Tomás left this morning at nine for the plane ride. Don't forget to meet him around three to find out about the shipments."

"No, I won't. Take care. See you in a few days." Paul hung up without saying anything else, and sat down, feeling a bit weak. He had never spoken to her with such distance. He guessed that he didn't trust her anymore. Hurt and alone, he wondered if she had been telling the truth about really wanting to leave Carlos. He ached to hold her in his arms, yet at the same time wanted to keep her away until he figured things out. Was she working with Mango instead of him? Did she trust Mango more by giving him the bank information? When he had called the State Department to ask who had taken over for Brian, he was told to follow Mango's orders until they contacted him again.

He picked up the phone and called the Treasury Department to ask them to investigate the bank that Gaby had visited, and told them to fax him any information. Then he left the hotel to rent a car. When he returned, he lunched on the hotel veranda and decided to take a few laps in the pool.

****

Tomás gazed down at all the activity on the river bank as the plane circled and came in to land. The little wheels dropped and they slowly skidded to a halt. He jumped out and walked over to the boats that were docked at the shore. Soon he heard shouts from men near the plane. They were unloading large crates onto a small truck from the back of the plane. The boy walked over and watched as the heavy crates went past him, and noticed a red and yellow stamp at the upper right corner of the crates. Inside the red circle, golden letters spelled out "Mirabelle." On the bottom, a jumble of letters and numbers in black ink decorated each box. Tomás concentrated and memorized the one going by. It was exactly the same on the next crate. "Mir610Cab."

****

Dripping a bit of pool water onto the thick grey carpets in the hallway, Paul rushed inside to take a shower before catching the bus to meet Gaby's brother. The whir of the fax machine lured him over and he waited for the paper to slowly emerge. Picking it up, he saw the emblem at the top telling him it was official State correspondence. One sentence appeared: "Banco de Crédito in Lima listed under Chairman of the Board of Directors: Jorge Rojas."

CHAPTER 31

Pushing the revolving door forward, Paul stepped out of the hotel and into the overcast mid-afternoon haze. He crossed the street and walked past the designer boutiques that lined the block where his hotel was located. The bus stop was only a few blocks away. He stopped and peered into the sparkling windows, eyeing the smart, colorful fashions and accessory displays while he lit a cigarette. As he clicked his lighter off, his eye caught someone across the street reflected in the glass. A man paced back and forth, pulling a newspaper from under his arm and then replacing it. Paul moved toward the door of the shop as if about to enter. The stranger waited, then crossed the street a bit farther down and ducked into a store.

As Paul passed the spot where he thought the man had entered, he saw no one near the entrance or inside the front of the shop. He walked on and crossed a side street. This block was not quite as elegant and the third one grew even less appealing, its storefront display windows cracked and covered with a dirty film, showing dusty, outdated dress styles which hung limply from broken mannequins.

Paul spotted the bus stop sign at the next corner and quickened his pace when he heard a bus approach from behind. As he turned to see what number it was, he noticed the man with the newspaper slowly walking along, stopping now and then to window shop.

This bus was not the one he needed to take, so he slowed down and waited for the stoplight. As he crossed the street and headed for the waiting area he heard footsteps behind him. Was he being paranoid or was this man really following him? Paul joined a woman holding a little girl on her lap and took a seat on the edge of the bench. The man turned down the side street away from the bus stop.

The air was moist and muggy, and the woman tried to cool the little girl with a pleated paper fan decorated with a Spanish flamenco dancer. He loosened his shirt collar and wiped his forehead with his handkerchief. The little girl smiled at him and then turned, hiding her face against her mother's shoulder.

Soon the bus wheels screeched and he looked up to see a crowded number 11, the one that would drop him off near the wharves. Allowing the woman and girl to climb on first, he glanced around to see if the stranger had come forward, but he saw no one. Jumping on, he shoved his ticket into the little machine behind the driver. Noticing that the bus was full, he grabbed the hanging strap and tried to stand so that he could shift his weight when the bus pulled out into traffic.

After a while, he saw the café through the window and began to push his way to the back to get off. The brakes screeched and he swung himself down and off the step and jumped to the sidewalk. There was no one sitting outside at the tables, so he entered the café and settled himself on one of the red leather stools, its upholstery slashed and cracked with coarse stuffing beginning to work its way out. Ordering a beer, he turned toward the front so he could watch for the brave boy. His watch told him it was just three o'clock. The bartender eyed him suspiciously, but continued wiping the table top and then began cutting some lime wedges for drinks. Paul spotted Gaby's little brother turning the corner. Picking up his beer and tossing some change down, he parted the glass beaded curtain that divided the sidewalk tables from the inside, and walked out to meet him.

"Well, Tomás, I see you made it back in one piece. How was your adventure?"

"It was great, Señor Brennan. You should have come with me!"

"Sit down here and I'll get you a Coke. Then you can tell me all about it."

Paul returned with the drink and Tomás took a long draw on the straw. His face was alive with discovery and excitement, and Paul wished at that moment he could turn back the clock so that he too could be twelve again, enjoying the simple pleasures of youth.

"Well?" Paul asked impatiently, as the boy gulped another mouthful of soda.

"We landed in Leticia and they began to unload the cargo…lots of crates. They told me they were orchids and fruits. The crates were put onto trucks and driven to the dock and put on the boat."

"Where was the boat headed?"

"Down the Amazon to Suriname."

"Did you notice anything else?"

"The crates all had the same stamp on them. They all said 'Mirabelle' on the top. At the bottom there were black letters with 'Mir610cab.'"

"Mir stands for the ship's name, and cab of course is Caballa," Paul thought to himself.

"Did the pilots say when the boat would arrive in Suriname?"

"No. But they said Uncle José would be home as soon as he delivers the money."

"Money? What money?"

Tomás looked quizzically at him and shrugged his shoulders. "Can I have another soda?"

"Sure. Can you remember anything else that was mentioned? What was the name of the boat they were loading?"

"The *Mirabelle*, of course! The sailors promised me a trip down the Amazon next time."

"Tell them you're not interested. It's too dangerous for you. I don't want you to get hurt. Your sister would never forgive me. You did very well. Here's some money for another Coke. Stay here awhile after I leave, will you?"

"Sure, Señor Brennan. And thanks!"

Paul got up and looked around. A faint breeze stirred the café's awning flap, but no one seemed to be looking at him. He waved good-bye to his little friend and took off down the street, crossing to the other side when he was out of Tomás's sight. He decided to walk a bit and catch the bus at a different stop.

The streets were silent and empty, enveloped by the relentless garua, which rolled in from the sea coating everything with its misty vapor like a grey veil. He had to get to a phone to call the paper. Perhaps his colleagues were the only ones he could trust now. They might be able to tell someone at the State Department to trap the *Mirabelle* at the other end of the river. As he walked along looking for a phone booth, he thought about the black code on each crate. Turning a corner, he saw a small grocery store and outside, an old-fashioned phone booth. Hoping it operated, he dug into his pockets for some coins. Picking up the moist receiver, he threw them down the telephone's throat and starred at graffiti scratched into the metal sides. Small hearts containing initials and dates decorated the inside of the booth, reminding him of one he had used in New York City. Kids were no different anywhere on earth, he thought. Paul dialed the number and waited. Then it came to him. The numbers 610 weren't quantities, but a date! June 10th! It came back to him. The blackboard in the warehouse! The shipment was probably due to leave Suriname on the tenth! Suddenly the phone stopped ringing and the line went dead.

"Hello! Hello!" he yelled a few times, then hung up in disgust. Leaving the phone booth he walked on, feeling sure he was near the bus stop. The damp air began to suffocate him and his eyes felt the sting of perspiration. He pulled out his handkerchief to wipe his face. Just then he heard footsteps behind him, walking in the same rhythm as his own. He stopped and the echo disappeared. He began to walk again, this time more slowly. There they were again! Should he turn around or go on as if he had heard nothing?

He suddenly turned down a narrow alley and started running, darting into a dark passage between two houses. He waited. Footsteps followed past his hiding spot. Breathing deeply, he pulled his gun from its holster and peered out. A short man in a suit walked hurriedly down the alley. Paul crept up on him and grabbed him from behind, throwing him against a stone fence and pushing him to the ground. Recognizing him as the man with the newspaper he had seen earlier, he shouted at him.

"Why are you following me? Who are you? *Habla inglese?*"

The man said nothing. Paul pointed the gun at him while he thrust his other hand down into the man's jacket pocket and pulled out some ID. The familiar US State seal on the card astounded him.

"You work for State?" he shouted.

"I was told to follow you, Mr. Brennan. Don't get so rough! I was only doing my job!"

"What's the matter? Haven't you ever stalked anyone before?" Paul asked him sarcastically, tossing the man's ID back to him as he got up off the ground.

"Who told you to follow me? For what purpose?"

"I have no idea why. I was just told to follow you and make a list of where you go and who you see."

"You must know more than that. You better tell me everything you know, right now, because this crazed killer you followed might decide to take your life. Did Mango send you?" Paul glared at him and twisted his arm behind his back, pushing the gun to his temple.

"No, please don't hurt me! I don't know any Mango. I was sent here by Brian Matthews. State wants you watched. They suspect that you are aiding the drug cartel and thwarting DEA efforts. That's all I know, I swear."

"Matthews has been dead for almost a week. Did you know that?"

"I take my orders from fax messages. All I know is that yesterday I received a note and it was signed by Matthews."

Paul pushed him aside. "Do you live here in Lima?"

"Yes, why?"

"Where's the nearest bus stop? I need to get back to the center of town."

"Two blocks up, then turn left." The man swung his arm toward the right to point the direction.

"Let's go there. We'll have a chance to talk while we're waiting."

Paul pushed him ahead, keeping his gun pinned at his back. How could State suspect him? Why would they even consider such a situation? Didn't they trust him? And who was signing Brian's name to fax messages? Or was he really alive?

CHAPTER 32

Paul pushed his way across the lobby, past groups of tourists and piles of suitcases and headed toward the bar.

"What's going on?" he shouted after he ordered a bottle of vodka and tonic and an ice bucket to be sent to his room.

"Convention attendees are leaving sir," the bartender replied. Paul tossed a few extra dollars down to make sure his order was delivered right away and took the elevator. Nearing the door, he took out his room key and pointed it toward the lock. He didn't need to use it. The door was ajar. Taking out his handkerchief, he covered the knob and pushed it a bit. Had the maid forgotten to lock it, or was she working inside? He pulled his gun out just in case he had company and slowly walked just inside past the door. Hearing no noise, he continued walking and saw that the room's contents had been turned upside down. The bedding was disheveled and drawers were pulled out. His suitcases had been dumped upside down and papers had been tossed on the floor. The phone began to ring and he covered the receiver with his handkerchief and picked it up.

"Brennan? This is Research. We are just calling to check if you received our fax."

"Fax? I just got in. Hold on." He tiptoed carefully across the mess and looked. There was nothing in the tray.

"Better send it again. Someone just ransacked my room and probably took it. When was it sent?"

"At 3:30 p.m."

"Listen, before you hang up, switch me to Dave on the international news desk will you? It's important."

"Sure, hold on."

"Dave? Is that you? It's Paul. Listen. Someone at State thinks I'm sabotaging the DEA's work. Someone followed me today and told me he was instructed to tail me. And they've searched my room. Can you find out what's going on for me?"

"Look, PB, I can't meddle in this very much. State tells *us* what to do, remember? But since you're such a good friend, I'll see what I can find out."

"The guy who tailed me told me he received a fax from Brian Matthews yesterday. I don't know what the hell is going on in Washington anymore!"

"Brian Matthews is definitely dead. They buried his body today. One of the girls covered the story. But I'll get her to scout around and let you know as soon as I hear anything."

"Tell her to hurry. I don't plan on staying here much longer, Dave. Things are getting very weird and dangerous."

"Research wants to know if you've got the fax turned on now."

Hearing the buzz of the machine, he said "Yeah, it's coming through now. Talk to you later, Dave."

Paul walked to the door and locked it. Then he phoned the reception desk.

"This is Mr. Brennan. I'll be checking out in the morning. Would you prepare my bill? And send a maid up. The room is a mess."

He walked over to the fax and picked up the sheet of paper and began to read:

Antonia Cenera born in Lima, 1961...convicted of petty street crime at age 15...married Maria Liguitas, a Bolivian...moved to Cuba in 1979 and divorced in 1983...went to Miami same year...recruited by CIA 1984...may have ties to organized crime in US...worked for US State Dept. since 1986...NOTE: We had trouble getting this much info...CIA and State unwilling to divulge more.

Just then he heard a knock at the door. His liquor had arrived and as he signed the bill and closed the door, a thought occurred to him. Why not call the DEA directly and tell them to be on the lookout for the *Mirabelle*? When they catch her in Suriname his name would hopefully be cleared. After pouring himself a drink, he gathered the papers together that were strewn about and closed his briefcase. There had to be a local contact in Lima, but who was it?

Grabbing the phone, he dialed Washington and was put through to the DEA. After several receptionists passed him over to minor officials, he was able to speak to the head of South American affairs.

"Look, I'm telling you to that my information is genuine. Trap the *Mirabelle* at Suriname and you'll find cocaine. She probably left Leticia sometime today. All the crates are stamped with a red circled "Mirabelle" at the top. On the bottom there is a code…"

"I'm sorry but we were told by State not to accept any information from you, Mr. Brennan."

"Well aren't you even going to check it out? The code stands for June tenth sailing of the *Mirabelle*. Find Caballa!"

"State seems to think you might be feeding us erroneous messages. I cannot forward this to any agents in South America."

"State doesn't know what the hell they're doing, damn it!" he shouted.

"Do you want me to relate that message, sir?" said a sarcastic voice.

Slamming the receiver down, he lit a cigarette and puffed furiously. What was going on? Why was someone trying to frame him? The knock at the door jarred him from his thoughts and he opened the door to let the maid in. Her face was aghast, and he pushed a five dollar bill into her hand to make the job a little sweeter.

"I'll take a shower now," he told her, pointing to the bathroom, and she seemed to understand as she tore the sheets off the bed and went out to the hall for fresh linens.

When Paul had finished his shower she had gone and everything was back in place. He shaved and dressed. Pulling on his jacket, he turned off the lights and closed the door. After a nice quiet dinner downstairs he would find that little jazz club he had wanted to enjoy with Gaby, in celebration of his last night in Peru.

CHAPTER 33

Soothing bossa nova rhythms began to calm his shattered nerves, and he sipped a cool rum drink in the shadows at a small side table, away from center stage. He focused on the spotlighted singer who sauntered among the guests, handing a rose to a recent wide-eyed bride, or throwing a kiss to a lonely old gentleman. How he wished things could have been different! If the bank hadn't been bombed, he and Gaby would have perhaps spent a wonderful romantic evening in this club, listening to songs which might have woven magic into their relationship, rendering it deeper and richer.

Instead, Paul sat alone, doubting that she had ever loved him. Why hadn't he questioned her more? Why hadn't he seen things for what they really were? Convincing himself that she'd never leave Carlos, he ordered another drink and tried to solve the puzzle. Were she and Mango working together or was Carlos masterminding this game? He knew she had lied to him at first about her father, but she had seemed so sincere. Perhaps she had never cared for him at all. Thinking about her now just made him angry and resentful.

The waitress brought his drink and he picked it up, eager to make himself numb to the hurt. His mind raced with questions. What about Washington? How much do they really understand? Do they believe a hoodlum like Cenera? How could he make them see what was going on in Lima and Bogotá? The only people he could trust were his colleagues at the newspaper office. Then it occurred to him! He could simply quit the government work and expose it all by writing articles. He had to extricate himself as soon as possible.

He decided that he would drive to the airport tomorrow morning, turn in the rental car, and take the first plane home.

The singer had finished and couples began to fill the dance floor and sway to the music, just as he and Gaby had done in his dream. He felt agitated and trapped. He couldn't stay any longer. Quickly paying his bill, he walked out into the cool night air.

As he drove home along crowded streets alive with pulsing movement and noise, he suddenly realized that he couldn't leave without knowing the truth from Gaby, without telling her how he felt and saying good-bye. He parked the car in the underground garage and decided to call her in the morning and visit her on his way to the airport.

The hotel lobby was strangely silent as he waited for the elevator; the quiet was so unlike all the frantic hours and days he had experienced there, that a kind of sadness wrapped itself around him. The click of the door lock brought him back to reality, and he pushed the door open.

The strong scent of her perfume instantly hit him! He flipped on the light switch.

"Paolo, I had to see you my darling!" She quickly came toward him, throwing her arms around him, showering him with kisses. For a moment he was shocked to see her. Then he regained his composure. Pulling her arms away from his neck, he pushed her away.

"Gaby, this is a surprise. I thought you were recuperating."

Her ashen face looked terrified, as if she suddenly understood what she had thought during their phone conversation.

"What is wrong my darling? What has happened? Tell me, please!"

"No, Gaby. You tell me what's been going on. No more lies— just the truth!"

"Paolo, you must believe me. You are my only hope now."

"What are you doing here, now, Gaby?" he said decisively as he slowly removed his jacket.

"You must help me to get away. Carlos knows I'm in Lima and is coming to get me. He knows that I have been helping you. Please, you must save me, darling." She moved stiffly toward him, holding out her arms. "I beg you, Paolo. We must get away!"

"We're not going anywhere until you tell me the whole story. And don't come near me!"

She settled back on the edge of the bed, letting her short beige coat fall from her shoulders, exposing her black knit dress which hid the bulky tape and dressings binding her ribcage.

Paul cleared his throat. "Now I understand why you and Mango were so friendly in Bogotá. You knew each other."

"Oh no, I never..." she began to protest.

"Look, you either tell me the entire truth, or you leave right now, Mrs. Rojas. You can explain it anyway you like to your husband, but don't ask me to help you unless you are completely honest." Paul turned to open his briefcase, taking out a miniature recorder.

"It all goes on the tape, Gabriella. So start talking."

"You can't do this to me Paolo. We love each other. We don't have time for this. We need to leave tonight, together."

"Make time for this, or we will never see each other after tonight. To start with, how about telling me who ransacked my room today?"

"I don't know."

"You haven't been straight with me right from the start, Gaby. What the hell was Cenera's picture doing in your wallet?" he demanded, beginning to lose his patience with her. He pulled a chair close to the bed and sat down.

Her face suddenly changed to show that she understood, and she lowered her eyes. Paul pushed the record button and shoved the tape player under her nose.

"I met Antonio Cenera in high school. He was the leader of a student organization...well I guess you could call it a gang. He was a good friend and he protected me. I never liked him as you imagine, Paolo. But I think he always hoped I would change my mind. Anyway, after my mother died, I didn't return to Lima and I didn't see him again, until Carlos brought him home to dinner one evening shortly after we were married. He and my husband are working together, Paolo. They made me draw you into this. I swear it! I didn't want to do it."

"Draw me into what?"

"They are working on some kind of a deal."

"What deal?" he pressed her.

"I don't know, my darling. They never told me very much about it."

"You told Mango and I that you knew a great deal about Carlos's business and could help us. Now you are saying that you weren't told details. What can I believe?"

She quickly slipped off the bed and came toward him, falling into his lap and burying her head on his shoulder.

"I told you to stay away!" he shouted as he twisted her arm behind her back and pushed her off his lap.

"You're hurting me, Paolo" she complained as he pulled his gun from beneath a pant leg and pointed it at her.

"You should be used to this treatment from Carlos. Now tell me the rest."

She took a deep breath. "Carlos is moving his cocaine operations out of Colombia. He and some others want to set up headquarters in Venezuela and Brazil. It was Mango's idea to find an American who worked for the DEA."

"Why?"

"I'm not sure. After I got you to deliver the letter I was told nothing. I swear it!"

"You mean they lured me into the game by using you and the story about the letter?"

"Yes. I was told to make you believe I needed you to get the message to my father. I didn't want to, but Carlos threatened to kill me if I didn't help him. I was so afraid."

"Antonio Cenera, alias Mango, is a traitor to his country. Couldn't you see what he was doing? He's involved in drug smuggling and probably tips off dealers so they don't get caught by US agents. I'm certain he's the mole that Brian suspected, and he wants to pin the blame on me! Maybe he had Brian killed. The DEA already suspects me. He's probably feeding them false information. Or are you the mole, Gaby?"

Paul looked into her eyes, hoping she would tell him the truth.

"Are you with them?" he demanded.

She looked up and blinked back tears.

"The day after I met you I begged Carlos to forget the plan. I didn't want to involve you. But I had no choice. You don't know how vicious Carlos can be. You don't understand how things work here, Paolo. I wish you did. Then you might understand how difficult it was for me to resist them."

"I don't want to understand this country anymore! It's a nightmare of killing and torture and selfish greed…ten-year-old kids being electrocuted by corrupt police…politicians who are really drug dealers…children being exploited and honest journalists kidnapped and tortured and killed!"

"Is it so different in New York, Paolo? We are only trying to exist the best way we know how. Poverty makes you lose all sense of perspective. We are a starving nation. People do almost anything to escape the emptiness of hunger. The drug trade is the only game in town."

"Well it doesn't have to be, Gaby. If people like you would work against it you might get to a better place."

"People like me? I'm married to a powerful and popular drug trafficker who controls people like the pieces on a chessboard. You don't see the intricate network that traps and tangles you in its web. Oh, Paolo, I'm so tired of it all."

"Then get out of it. Leave Carlos. Leave Colombia. Don't you see you're drowning in this kind of life?"

She lowered her head and spoke in a low murmur.

"I'm so ashamed of what I have done to you, my darling. No matter what happens, believe that I love you." She pulled on her coat and pushed herself off the bed, moving toward the door.

"Gaby, wait. Don't go back to him. Stay here tonight. I'm leaving in the morning. I had planned to see you at your aunt's house before I caught the plane."

She turned and looked at him as if she wasn't quite sure what to believe anymore.

"I'm not sure it's safe to stay here much longer, Paolo. I'm afraid that Carlos will find us here."

"Then we'll leave in a few hours, before it gets light. I have to pack and pay my bill."

"Then you mean you'll take me with you?"

Her vulnerability and childlike hopefulness tugged at Paul's heart but he still wasn't willing to trust her completely. What if she was working with Carlos and this was a set up? What if she was sent to trap him? He couldn't take any chances now, but he hadn't made up his mind about his next move.

"Look, make yourself a drink and rest while I pack. I'm still not convinced that you're telling me everything you know. Are you still determined to leave Carlos and help to put him out of business?"

"I told you before that I do not want to be part of Carlos's drug business or part of his family. But I do have to think about my father and brother. They are important to me."

Paul shoved some shirts and socks into an empty suitcase. "The US government can help free your family if you cooperate. What else do you know about what Mango was doing?"

"Several months ago, Carlos told me that Mango would not be meeting with him as much for a while. When I asked why, he just said Mango had to be careful until he could arrange things so that he could move more freely and begin working in Brazil...or maybe it was Mexico...I don't remember. My husband promised to buy us a place on the ocean where we could get away."

"Yes, after Mango pulled me in and fed me to the sharks in Washington so he could continue to work with Carlos. Are you willing to testify against your husband?"

Gabriella quietly leaned back on the pillow and sipped her drink.

"If I am fortunate enough to be alive after all of this, and if it would stop the killing and torture, I would. But I don't think putting one man out of the drug smuggling business will change things. Carlos is devious. He has many friends who could help him run the business, even if he was in jail."

"The DEA would try and have him extradited to the US." Paul packed the fax and unplugged the computer. "What kind of life do you want for your father and brother? Would they be willing to leave South America?"

"My father is too old to start over somewhere else. I just want to give him a few peaceful years before he dies. Tomás is young and has a chance at a positive future, but only if he gets away from here."

Collecting his few shaving articles from the bathroom, Paul yelled, "What about your uncle? How heavily do you think he is involved in all this?"

"I only found out about my uncle the day of the bank bombing. I don't know exactly what he does for Carlos, but he certainly plays a part in the transfer of money or drugs or both."

"You mean money laundering?"

"I'm not sure about that, but I think my uncle uses his friend's orchid shipments to hide drugs. He brings my aunt an orchid once a month and told her that it was his bonus payment for helping his friend the florist. My aunt's favorite flower was the dark purple orchid because that was the flower my uncle gave her on their first date."

Paul walked back to Gabriella and stood beside her. She gazed up into his eyes like a naughty puppy, hoping for comfort but acting as if she didn't deserve it. Paul sat down on the bed and took her hand.

"So he is sending cocaine out in boxes of dark orchids, huh? Look, Gaby, until my government stops believing the lies that Mango is apparently feeding them, I can't help anyone. But as soon as I can, I'll help you and your family. I promise."

She raised her dark eyes in grateful acknowledgement and pressed her head against his arm.

"I only hope it won't be too late, my darling."

"I finished packing. Mango expects us to go to your father's ranch while he is in Washington. Let's not disappoint him."

"You mean you want to take me there?"

"Yes. In a few hours we're going to lead my watchdogs exactly where they think I plan to go. If my idea works, we could trap Carlos there."

"But how? Carlos is probably on his way here now in his jet!"

Paul put his arms around her shoulders.

"Gaby, don't be afraid of Carlos. I'll protect you. I promise."

She reached up and clasped her hands around his waist.

"I love you, Paolo" she whispered softly into his ear, and he rolled across the bed and cradled her in his arms, trying not to press against her side. As their lips met, he again felt the warmth of her charm that had so mesmerized him the day he met her on French cap. He closed his eyes and tried to hear the splash of the waterfall and feel the sun on his back. He slipped her blouse up and over her face, and reached up to turn off the light. He wanted to be with her once more, to feel her love surround him, and to let his love comfort her. He thought perhaps their dreams would help them face the reality that would surely meet them in a few hours.

CHAPTER 34

Gaby drifted off into a fitful sleep, and Paul got up, not able to sleep. Taking the tape recorder into the bathroom, he rewound it and played the tape, making sure he had all he needed. Their first stop out of town would be the newspaper office. They could express mail the tape to his colleagues in New York. He quickly made a duplicate and hid it in his luggage.

Glancing at his watch and seeing it was almost three a.m., he dressed and quietly moved the luggage out to the hallway. The elevator whisked him to the lobby where he paid his bill and packed the car.

When he returned to the room, Gaby was awake and had bathed. She emerged from the bathroom, her hair swept up and tucked back behind her ears lending a regal air to her little round face. He caught her in an embrace and gazed into the sharp, sultry eyes that glared back at him.

"I thought you had left without me, Paolo!"

"Never!" he whispered, and kissed her cheek. She gave him a voluptuous grin and turned away to finish dressing.

"I paid the bill and checked out, and the car is packed except for the equipment. Did you bring any bags?"

"No, I was afraid my aunt would be suspicious and hear me packing. All I have is a small overnight case with a change of clothes."

"Then carry the recorder, would you? I can handle the computer and fax."

She threw her coat over her arm and grabbed the tape recorder and her little bag and they closed the door.

"Do you know the way out of town, Paolo?"

"I can get to the highway that runs along the ocean. But first we will stop in town to drop something off."

She looked puzzled but said nothing and settled herself into the front seat and rolled the window down halfway. They drove slowly through the dark, empty streets toward the business district.

"I've never seen Lima so quiet," she murmured and then closed her eyes.

Paul found the news office and parked the car down the street.

"I'll only be a moment. Then we can be on our way."

"Be sure this goes out this morning to Dave Cummins on the Overseas Desk in New York. It's very important. Can I use your computer to send an email to New York? Thanks." Paul tapped out a quick message to Dave, explaining the tape and asking that he print a story about it if he turned up missing or dead.

Gaby had fallen asleep while she waited for him, and he put the car in gear and drove slowly toward the outskirts of town. When he reached the coastal highway, she woke up.

"You can only follow this a little way before you must turn off into the interior."

"Feeling better now?" he asked.

"I won't feel better until I can return to my father. I worry about him." Paul reached over and pressed her hand to try and soothe her, but she only turned away and tried to get back to sleep.

The rough ocean breakers tried to force their way onto the flat, dry desert, and for miles all Paul could see were dark mounds of sand on both sides of the road. This barren dead stretch of land seemed so empty and still in contrast to the pulsating waves beating the shore, which lay alongside the desert, as if life and death were fighting each other to take control of this weary, battle-scarred country.

"How soon do I turn, Gaby?"

She opened her eyes and looked around for a second or two. "About five miles more I think, Paolo. You'll see a sign for the main road that goes inland toward the Huallaga River. I'll watch for you."

It was still dark when Paul turned left onto a rutted, two-lane road that was poorly lit. Strange animals and shadows flared up into the headlights, and he slowed down.

"The driving will get easier when you reach the river. It will be on your left." Somehow she sensed that Paul was uneasy. "Trust me, Paolo," she added, with a squeeze to his right arm, and her words seemed to put him at ease. He began to think about how they had been thrown together and whether they would ever have a chance to build a life together.

"Isn't it strange...the two of us, a journalist from the US and the Peruvian wife of a Colombian drug king, in this faraway jungle trying to stay alive? We are both being pursued, you by your husband, me by my government, and we're the ones who are innocent! They committed the crimes, not us! We only want to see justice done."

"We also wanted to love each other a little, don't you think, Paolo? And this jungle isn't so far away to me. It used to be my home. But you are right. We don't want to belong to their world."

"What will become of you, my dear Gabriella? If only we had met before you married Carlos."

She sighed and looked out of the window.

"Sometimes I think love is better when it happens suddenly between two strangers and they don't stay together. It can be nurtured privately in each heart, where one cannot destroy it for the other."

"I wish we had brought some food," Paul remarked. "We've had no breakfast and we are going to be pretty hungry soon. It's starting to get light, and I finally see the river."

"There used to be a small village not far from here with a café. We could at least get bread and coffee before going to my father's ranch."

Paul continued to drive past thick, green, overgrown brush with huge pointed leaves that reached out onto the road. Tall trees hung overhead, their branches trying to mingle with the plants beneath them. Birds began to call to their mates, swooping up out of the interior and into the grey sky over the river, in search of some breakfast. An old man on a horse pulling a wagon-load of coffee beans passed and stared at the car with a strange, frightened expression.

"The village is just up ahead. If you don't slow down you'll miss it." Paul downshifted and slowed to a crawl. Several dilapidated buildings were clustered on the right, and the old café Gaby had mentioned was farther down the road.

Paul parked the car on the side of the little house whose front room served as the restaurant, and they walked over to the thatched-roof porch and up the two steps. Gaby peered into the dust covered window and tried the door. It was locked. She knocked a few times and yelled some Spanish words. A dog came up behind Paul, sniffing at his heels and then whining. Suddenly, he noticed someone looking out from the side of the house. The old man called to the dog, and the animal obediently ran toward him. Paul tapped Gaby's back and she turned around to see the bent old farmer, his threadbare blanket slung over his shoulder, his eyes wary and doubtful.

"I think I know this man," she said in a whisper, and called out to him, apparently explaining what they wanted. He shuffled to the front door and rapped on the glass, calling for Theresa to open the café. After a tired-looking woman unlocked the door, they stepped in and smelled the strong, sweet odor of fresh coffee. Gaby ordered two large steaming cups from the old woman who had emerged from the back room, and Paul sat down at a tiny table against the wall.

"She'll bring us some fresh bread soon," Gaby told him, and she joined Paul at the table. "They've lived here since I was a little girl, but it has been so long I don't think they remember me."

The old woman cautiously carried the two mugs of coffee over to them while holding a round loaf of bread under her arm. She placed the bread between the cups and Paul dug into his pocket for some change. At the sight of the money she brightened a bit, and

Gaby started a conversation, asking her if she remembered her father Ricardo.

Just then the door opened and a young man, dressed in military fatigues, burst in, throwing his gun on the only other table in the room and snapping his fingers. He sat down, planting his muddy boots on the chair across from him. The woman stopped talking to Gaby and addressed the soldier.

"Is he Peruvian army or revolutionary guerilla?" Paul asked Gaby quietly, while he gulped down the strong drink and tore off a large piece of warm bread.

Gaby put her cup down. "I don't know, but I think we shouldn't stay here long. It doesn't really matter which side he's on. You know that in this area these groups collaborate."

The soldier heard her speaking in English and got up. He came over and stared at Gabriella. Then he began to speak to her in Spanish and she answered him. He looked at Paul suspiciously and went back to his table.

"What did he want?"

"He asked me what I was doing here, since he could tell I was from the city. I told him I used to live here and was bringing some materials to my father's ranch."

"Materials? You mean…"

"I don't know what I meant, Paolo. I had to tell him something. He seems satisfied. He probably thinks I work for the men who run Carlos's operation up there. Let's get going!"

She grabbed what was left of the loaf and Paul drained the last drop of his coffee and quickly stood up. The soldier looked up and watched them go out the door.

"How much farther to your father's land?" Paul said as he put the car in gear.

"You mean Carlos's property…maybe less than an hour, maybe more. What is the plan?"

"Did I say I had a plan? We'll see if we can get through the guards, which I'm sure are stationed at the entrance. You are not to leave my sight, darling. Just tell the guards you wanted to show me around. If they are Carlos's men they should know who you are."

"And if he told them to take you prisoner?" she countered.

"I don't think they'll do that if I hold a gun to your head."

Gaby suddenly became indignant. "So you are going to use me as a shield?"

"*You* used *me*, didn't you? Look, I love you Gaby, but I want to get out of here alive. If you want to come with me, it's up to you. You have an hour to make up your mind. If my message gets through, the DEA forces at the base camp might be able to get here in time and trap Carlos. If they're successful, you can come back with me to the States."

"And if the DEA doesn't show up, or you are unsuccessful?"

"I haven't thought that far ahead yet. Maybe you can complete the scenario."

"Oh, I can easily complete it. Carlos's men will take you prisoner and probably shoot you, and I'll be returned to Bogotá, where my husband will punish me in ways you can't even imagine."

Paul glanced at her face and knew she was right. He was taking a big chance with both their lives, but he wanted to clear his name and put Mango and Carlos in DEA custody if he could possibly do it. He also wanted to give Gaby a chance to get away from Carlos forever if that was what she wanted.

He drove on through the countryside. Gaby was silent. Then she spotted a familiar area and became alive with nostalgia. Pointing out places she recognized, she became more animated than he had ever seen her before. These were her roots, and her childhood home had a place in her heart that could never be displaced. Her eyes glowed as she looked down over the gently rolling hills where coffee beans had once matured under her father's watchful gaze.

"There is my special spot where I would hide from the world!" she exclaimed. "And there is where my brothers used to meet the boys from the next village, where sisters were not admitted!" she shouted excitedly, pointing to a little hut used to store bean baskets. Paul turned a corner and drove closer to the house and she suddenly became silent. She looked past the clustered buildings Carlos had erected to prepare shipments of coca to Colombia for processing. She lowered her head and crossed herself.

"On the little hill right behind that building my mother is buried."

Paul slowed the car and approached the gate. Four guards holding machine guns appeared from behind the two huge stone gateposts. Paul held his breath.

"Tell them we were told to meet Carlos here, and make it sound convincing."

CHAPTER 35

The guards quickly surrounded the car and motioned for them to get out. As Gaby began to explain, one of the guards searched the car and pointed to the trunk. Paul opened it, and the guard removed his suitcase and fax.

"He wants you to open it, Paolo," Gaby shouted, as one of the guards began to frisk her. Paul dug for the key in his wallet and flung the top open, hoping the guard wouldn't find the extra tape. After rummaging a bit he felt satisfied and pushed Paul up against the car to see what weapons he carried. Fortunately he had stashed his gun in a hidden compartment deep in the suitcase.

The guards waved them through and Paul drove slowly up the winding stone driveway. He heard the heavy iron gates clang shut behind them.

"Today I am being respected as the wife of Carlos Rojas," Gaby said sarcastically, as she pushed her hair out of her eyes. "They told me he is on his way here. Apparently he hasn't told them that I work for the enemy, unless they are playing a game with us."

"Where shall I put the car?"

"Just follow the little road to the left of the house. It winds up the hill a bit. Park it heading downhill on the other side so it can't be seen from the gate. If you need to get away fast, drive down a little way until you reach a dirt road. Turn right and drive between the trees until you come to the next village."

After Paul retrieved his gun from the suitcase, they got out and climbed back up to the ridge, where they could view the property. Gaby gasped and clung to Paul's arm.

"Oh, Paolo, I had forgotten how beautiful my father's land is. Look at all of this!" She swept her arm out across the landscape, pointing to the house with the veranda where her father must have watched many sunsets.

"Now I understand why it hurt your father so much to leave," and Paul put his arm around her. "I can also see why Carlos wanted it. Whoever owns this area commands the valley."

"The soil is rich and the climate perfect," she said in a low voice as she turned to take it all in. "My father often told me he hoped one day to sit on the veranda watching his grandchildren play while he sipped his espresso. I never gave him that opportunity. None of us did." Then she focused on a spot behind the house and became silent.

"Let's go down while we still have time. I want to show you the house I grew up in."

Paul took her hand and they slowly made their way down the little path worn into the ground by countless numbers of feet on their way to the Santiago household. A guard stood on the far side of the veranda, and Gaby cautiously mounted the few steps. He didn't approach them, and she led Paul to the front door. She tried the door but it was locked tight. Gabriella called to the guard and asked him to open it.

"Not until Señor Rojas gets here," he replied as he walked toward them.

Gaby turned a tearful face away from the guard as she led Paul toward the back of the house.

"If I can't show you the inside of the house, we can visit Mother," she suddenly announced in a low voice, like a child who had been hurt and needed to retaliate.

She briskly walked away, past the prefabricated shacks that Carlos had erected to store the packages waiting to be shipped north. Turning a corner behind one of them, she knelt down and crossed herself. As Paul came closer, he could see part of a metal bar sticking out of the moist earth, and some broken pieces of stone which once formed a carved headstone. Gaby ran her outstretched fingers across the R of her mother's first name, and began to speak in low tones, counting the black rosaries she had pulled out of her pocket. Then she started to sob, and Paul knelt down beside her and pulled her toward him.

"Don't," he whispered. "She forgives you, whatever you may have done." She turned to him and pressed her head into his shoulder.

"If only we had some flowers," she cried, and he looked behind them hoping to spot something to place on the grave.

"Mother always loved the color yellow," Gaby murmured as she pulled a bright orange-red scarf from her coat pocket. "Perhaps this will do," she said as she tied it around the rusted metal which was once a gleaming, cross-shaped grave marker. Paul pulled her up to her feet and pushed her hair out of her eyes. Then he took her in his arms and kissed her trembling lips.

Suddenly they heard the sound of approaching cars and moved to where they could see the gate. Carlos's entourage had arrived. Paul quickly pushed Gaby ahead of him away from the shacks and up the hill into a protected area, behind a cluster of bushes. Pulling his revolver out, he positioned her in front of him.

"Paolo, what are you doing?"

"Just a little security for both of us. If Carlos wants you, he'll have to give in to my demands."

"And what do you want from him?"

"I want him to tell the DEA about working with Mango and explain to them that it wasn't me. And to give you up, if that's what you want."

"He'll never do it, Paolo."

"Maybe he won't have any choice if the US forces get here in time. Stay down!"

Paul raised himself up just enough to see Carlos strutting around talking to his guards. Then the second car door opened and Mango jumped out, slamming the door and gesturing wildly to Carlos, shouting something Paul couldn't understand.

"Mango's here. So he was lying about flying to DC."

"It sounds like they are arguing," Gaby said as he pushed her back down.

"They're coming toward us Gaby. Are you staying with me or going back to your husband?"

"Gabriella, come down here!" Carlos commanded, and for an instant Paul felt her body inch slightly forward toward her husband as a reflex to his order. Paul waited until Carlos came a bit closer. Then he pushed Gaby to her feet and shoved the revolver into her temple.

"If you want your wife back in one piece, you better listen to me Carlos!" he shouted.

"Come down to the house where we can all talk, PB," he answered.

"*No*! The time for talking is over. You tell Mango I know he double-crossed me. If you don't promise to tell the DEA he's working with you, you'll never see your wife again."

"You're crazy, Paul. We're working on the same side!" shouted Mango as he also began walking up the hill.

"You mean you and Carlos are working on the same side. You tried to get Washington to believe I was the traitor!"

"My guards are coming up to get you both!" Carlos shouted.

"If they come any closer I'll blow her head off."

Gaby began to struggle and he held her tight against his body. Carlos backed away and began speaking to Mango and the guards again. Then he looked up toward them.

"Her life isn't worth mine, Carlos. She used me just like you and Mango did. She was part of this too!"

"She had nothing to do with it, believe me. It was between Mango and me. Listen. I'll speak to your superiors about Mr. Cenera. I was ready to cut him loose anyway. Just allow Gabriella to come down to me."

"Not yet. There's one more demand. Gabriella wants to come with me. She's had enough of you, Carlos. Your wife wants asylum in the US."

"Let me hear her say that. Is it true, Gabriella?"

Gaby hesitated and couldn't speak.

"Tell him what you want to do, Gaby. I won't kill you," he whispered. "I just need to trap Mango and turn him over to the DEA."

"I don't believe my wife would want to put her dear father and brother in danger…would you, Gabriella?"

Gaby trembled and peered over the top of the bushes. One of the guards opened the limo door and pushed Tomás roughly toward Carlos, who put his arm around the boy.

"Oh, Paolo, now I can't go with you. God did not mean for us to be together."

"He's only bluffing, Gaby. He wouldn't hurt your little brother. Think what you are giving up. You may never have another chance. Don't go back to him! I love you!"

"Vaya con Dios, my love" she whispered. All of a sudden Paul heard someone behind him. As he turned to see Mango lunging at him, he loosened his grip and Gaby broke free and ran toward Tomás.

Mango grabbed Paul's arm and pressed him to the ground, smashing his wrist against the ground. The revolver flew out of his hands and Paul pushed his knee into Mango's chin, swinging his fist against his jaw. Punching him again, Paul tried to get up but couldn't reach the gun. Mango shook his head and then got up and headed toward his prey. Out of the corner of his eye, Paul saw two guards with guns raised, heading up the hill. Suddenly he felt a blow to his head and for an instant he couldn't see clearly. Then he spotted the revolver and dove for it. Grabbing the cold steel handle, he turned it toward Mango.

"Don't come closer or I'll shoot you, Mango!"

Mango kept coming, so Paul pulled the trigger, his head throbbing and beating. A shot rang out. Mango reeled and spun to the ground, holding his shoulder and grimacing in pain. As Paul came toward him and leaned down, Mango's left arm flashed upward, a sharp knife gripped in his fingers ready to stab Paul in the leg. Paul kicked it out of Mango's grip.

"Just stay where you are, Mango, or I'll use this again closer to your heart." Then he turned the gun toward the two guards who had made it to the hilltop. "You want to be next?" he shouted. With that, they heard Carlos calling for help and they ran back down the hill.

Hearing the whirring of helicopter blades, they all looked up to see two US choppers landing near the house. Paul could see Carlos twisting Gaby's arm behind her, pushing her toward the limo while she struggled and kicked to get free. Two other guards had taken up a position against the house and aimed their guns at the DEA forces. Paul sank back down on the ground, not wanting to be caught in a cross fire. Pulling his handkerchief out of his back pocket while keeping his gun trained on Mango, he pressed it to his forehead to stop the bleeding.

Shots rang out and one of Carlos's guards fell. Men from the second helicopter ran toward the limo and the sky turned a smoky purple as exploding grenades and then teargas filled the air, causing the birds to scatter up into the morning mist which was just beginning to burn off as the sun pushed its way upward.

Paul looked down at the grave, where the orange scarf fluttered in the gentle, damp breeze, a mother trying to bid farewell to the daughter she had lost so long ago. He shuddered, as if some strange hand of fate was trying to warn him of impending doom.

When he heard the voices of DEA agents calling his name, he knew it was safe to go down.

CHAPTER 36

"Hey, Brennan, don't work so hard! Ever since you got back from South America you've been killing yourself. Don't you know it's Friday night?"

"It wouldn't hurt if you put in some overtime, Joe. Your rewrites have been lousy and you take too many two-hour martini lunches."

"Seriously, Paul, what happened to you down there? You certainly don't seem the same to me."

Suddenly Dave came to his rescue, and he turned back to the computer to finish editing his report.

"Paul just needs to work some things out, Joe. Why don't you go down to O'Neal's ahead of us and order a drink. We'll join you later."

"Thanks, Dave," Paul muttered as he added the final touches to his story.

"You know, he's right, don't you? You are spending a lot of time here. You've been back for almost six months and I still haven't heard the whole story. I'm worried about you, Paul."

"Nothing to worry about my friend...I'll be fine. I'll tell you all about it tonight over a glass of red wine."

"It's the girl, isn't it...the one who is married to Rojas?"

"Meet you in a half hour at O'Neal's, Dave. I've got to check on the foreign wire service releases that should be in by now. I promise I'll be there soon."

Dave raised his eyebrows and pointed his finger at him as if to say you better keep your word, and walked down the hall.

Tapping the enter key, Paul sent his final draft to the wrap file, and called up the program for the overseas reports. Kashmir, Thailand, Berlin, Yeltsin...the same boring reports as yesterday, he thought. Maybe Joe and Dave were right. Perhaps throwing himself into his work wasn't helping.

He hit the exit key and got up. Walking past several computers that had been left on in the research division, a flash caught his eye, and he stopped to stare at one of the screens. A fresh release was just being frantically typed in from far away. He began to turn away when he noticed the origination box at the top of the screen. The writer was spelling Medellín. He had to read this!

The story covered the recent search for Escobar and his friends. Then it went on to give some background for readers not familiar with the drug kingpin's history. Other cartel heads were mentioned in the final section. Then the name Rojas appeared, and his heart skipped a beat. He sat down and continued to read.

Carlos Rojas, leader of a rival drug faction, was paroled today after serving a five-month sentence. He returned to his palatial home on the outskirts of Bogotá, where he had lived with his parents and other family members. Last week his wife was found murdered in Lima, and some speculate that he engineered her death from his prison cell, as revenge for finding out that she was involved with US drug enforcement agents. Mr. Rojas's father denied the charge, claiming that she was a victim of political revolutionaries who want to overthrow the government and attack the Rojas family, which has many ties to influential leaders.

There was nothing further. No date of her death, no mention of how she was murdered. His heart ached and he began to choke.

Then her words slowly tumbled back to him, her voice a soft, gentle whisper.

"We must be strong when we are apart, Paolo." Then in a sadder tone, "Love is better when it happens suddenly between two strangers and they don't stay together. It can be nurtured privately in each heart where one can't destroy it for the other."

That's what we'll do from now on, Gaby, Paul thought, trying to console himself.

Our love will be safe that way, from Carlos, from government meddling, from anything or anyone. He let out a muffled sob and searched for his handkerchief.

Wiping a tear from his eye, he got up and turned off the computer. As he listened to the slow tones of the hard drive winding down and shutting off, she spoke to him once more from the past.

"Paolo, I can't go with you. God didn't mean for us to be together. No matter what happens, believe that I love you."

"Vaya con Dios, my Gabriella," he whispered. "I hope you are finally at peace."

THE END